★ THE SECRET BOX ★

Books by Gayle Pearson

Fish Friday
The Coming Home Cafe
One Potato, Tu
The Fog Doggies and Me
The Secret Box

THE ★ SECRET ★ BOX

GAYLE PEARSON
· · · · · · · · · · · · · · · · · · ·

A JEAN KARL BOOK

Atheneum Books for Young Readers

For Laurie

Atheneum Books for Young Readers
An imprint of Simon & Schuster Children's Publishing Division
1230 Avenue of the Americas
New York, New York 10020

Book design by Nina Barnett
The text of this book is set in 13-point Bembo.

First Edition
Printed in the United States of America
10 9 8 7 6 5 4 3 2 1

Library of Congress Cataloging-in-Publication Data
Pearson, Gayle.
The secret box / Gayle Pearson.—1st ed.
p. cm.
"A Jean Karl book."
Summary: A trip to San Francisco's Chinatown, a dog's funeral, and a
shoplifting incident reveal some previously unknown "secrets" and
affect the relationships between twelve-year-old Taylor and thirteen-
year-old Lindsey and their respective older brothers.
ISBN 0-689-81379-1
[1. Brothers and sisters—Fiction. 2. Conduct of life—Fiction.] I. Title.
PZ7.P32312   Se 1997
[Fic]—dc20
96-30459

CONTENTS

· · · · · · · · · · · ·

THE SECRET BOX

Taylor Finch drew back the filmy white curtain and peered out at the faded blue Plymouth parked in front. She felt sneaky doing it, spying on Rudy Garch like this, but she couldn't help it. Someday she'd get caught, maybe by her brother, maybe by Rudy himself. She turned red just thinking about it and let go of the curtain.

Thump thump. Her brother, Toby, was clumping around his room upstairs in his heavy black boots. Soon he'd march down the stairs and out the front door and go off with Rudy. Then she'd be alone again. Her mom was at the hospital, where she worked as an aide. The work was hard, and she would come home tired.

Taylor carefully parted the curtain again. One last look at Rudy, his long, lanky body folded up behind the steering wheel, his Oakland A's cap tilted back on his head like he owned the world. God, he was cool!

Beeeeeeeeeeeeeep. She jumped as he blasted the horn, then darted across the living room and tore up the stairs, two at a time. She burst into her bedroom and slammed the door shut behind her, giggling into the palm of her hand as she gave the door a final push with her butt.

Whew! That was a close call. Someday she would get caught spying and have to admit it. Admit what? she said to herself. That she had a crush on Rudy Garch? Rudy Garch! She threw herself face down on her bed with a loud groan. Love was going to be painful.

Now she heard Toby, lumbering down the hallway past her room. He was lucky, going off with Rudy Garch like it was nothing at all. She lay there waiting, hoping the sound of his footsteps would stop at her doorway and he'd have something to say. Like, What're you up to today? Or, You want to do something later? But he kept on walking, the way he always did now. She raised herself up on her elbows. "Hey, Toby!" she called.

She listened to the sound of his boots pounding the stairs. "What?" he hollered back a few seconds later, from somewhere down near the bottom.

"Where are you going?" she called.

"Out!" he hollered. Then the front door slammed shut behind him.

"Out," she repeated aloud to herself. "Well, big deal." Then it got real quiet. She pulled at a loose thread in the bedspread, straining to hear Rudy's old Plymouth revving up and pulling away from the curb but she couldn't. It was just quiet and nothing else.

She sat up and tapped out a few beats of a song with

her fingers on her knee, wondering what to do next. Television? Homework? Call somebody on the phone? She glanced at the stack of books and notebooks on the table beside her bed and made a face. She just wasn't in the mood, and she shouldn't have to sit here doing homework when other people were out having fun.

She reached for one of the notebooks and skipped through it until she came to an empty page. *Taylor Finch,* she wrote in the upper left-hand corner, and then *RG RG RG RG RG,* in neat letters across the top of the page. Underneath it she drew a picture of the faded blue Plymouth, Rudy behind the wheel with his cap tilted back. *I have a crush on RG,* she scrawled underneath it. *He is the cutest guy I've ever seen.* She liked writing it down, liked seeing the words looking back at her from the paper.

On the next page she drew a close-up of Rudy's face, as best she could remember it. She was not a very good drawer. That had never bothered her before, but now it was disappointing. The face on the page was not Rudy. Rudy was cute and funny and he had a great haircut. You couldn't see any of that in the drawing. The face was too long, like the head of a horse, and the horse did not have a great haircut.

The hair was blue instead of brown but that wasn't her fault. She was using a blue pen.

She tore the two pages from the notebook and got up to hide them. But where? In the back of her sock drawer? Imagine Toby ever getting his mitts on something like that! No, it wasn't safe enough. What she needed was a truly secret place, a place under lock and key.

She had just turned twelve, and her birthday presents were still stacked on her dresser: a long-sleeved yellow shirt from her dad, who lived in Albany; a flashlight from her younger brother, Timothy, who lived with her dad; an Oakland A's nightshirt and a Scrabble game from her mom; a watercolor set from her aunt Jackie; a RapSure tape from her cousin, Sudie; a sweater-and-pants set from her gramma and grampa; ten bucks from Toby; and a Chinese puzzle box from her aunt Bernadette. It was a lot of stuff. And she liked getting it.

She kept her presents on her dresser to make her birthday last longer. If she wore something, she just put it back in the box it came in. If she played with the game or the watercolors, she put them back on her bureau, too. She did the same thing at Christmas, keeping her presents under the tree until New Year's Day was over.

She pursed her lips in concentration, then picked up the Chinese puzzle box, turning it over a few times in her hand. The puzzle box was oval shaped and made of a thin, light wood, like the kind used in making model airplanes. The box was covered with red and gold Chinese letters. What the letters said was a mystery to Taylor. Another mystery was what the puzzle box looked like on the inside, because she had not yet figured out how to open it. When she'd begun to read the set of secret instructions on her birthday, she only got as far as the first paragraph, and then she groaned out loud. It said there were thirty-four secret steps to follow in opening the box. Thirty-four steps! It would take her all day.

Only now she really needed the box.

She removed the list of secret instructions from inside the plastic wrapping and began to reread them. "Slide the top wooden slat to the right and the bottom slat to the left. Slide the center and bottom slats both to the right and then to the left."

It was very confusing. She had to read each direction several times, and even then she wasn't sure she was doing it right.

"Slide the end slat with the silver circle once to the left, and the end slat with the red circle. Then slide the middle top slat back and forth three times and the right top slat back and forth two times." Whew! She was halfway through the thirty-four steps. Was she doing it right? Was it going to work?

After step thirty-three she lay the puzzle box down on her bed and took a deep breath. She could see how you could get real fast once you did it a few times, but now it had taken her nearly twenty minutes. She took another deep breath, because the last step should open the puzzle box, and she wondered if it would. She carefully lifted the large slats at each end of the box and—it was like a little miracle—off came the cover.

Inside, the box was bright yellow, the color of mustard. She stuck her nose into the box and sniffed. It didn't smell like mustard. It smelled new and fresh, like the brand-new house her friend Deirdre had just moved into. It smelled like new wood. She turned the box over in her hands, thinking maybe it was the best present she'd ever received, this secret box that was hers and nobody else's.

She folded the two sheets of paper into neat little

squares and tucked them away inside the puzzle box. She put the lid back in place, lowered the slats on each side, and bingo! Now her secret was safe! She left the box sitting out in plain view on her dresser, but she didn't have to worry. She'd folded the sheet of instructions in half and taped it onto the back of her bureau.

She felt awfully happy just then. She knew she could feel just about anything and write just about anything and there was a private place to put it all.

It was four fifteen. Her mom wouldn't be home until five thirty and there was no telling about Toby. She picked up her social studies book and went downstairs to read about the Aztec Indians.

"I wish I was fifteen, like you," Taylor said to Toby one morning at breakfast. "Twelve is going to be boring. I can already tell." She knew it wasn't true as soon as she said it. It wasn't going to be boring at all, and she'd only said it to impress him. But it didn't. He rolled his eyes and went on scooping up his cereal.

The truth was, eleven had sounded really young to her and twelve did not. Twelve sounded different, as though it could open up a whole world of possibilities, of magnificent opportunities. Why, she knew a twelve-year-old girl who was a model. She knew of a twelve-year-old girl who was a championship horseback rider. She also knew a twelve-year-old girl from school who'd just been sent to juvenile hall for . . . she couldn't remember exactly, but that was a horse of a different color, as her mom sometimes said.

The point was, she was twelve and that meant that she too could be a model or an athlete or something entirely different, and what would Rudy think of her then!

About the time Taylor finally decided to put her birthday presents away, her mother gave her one of those books about what it was like to "grow up," the things that would happen whether you liked it or not. Taylor didn't mind the chapters about dating and getting along with your parents. In the chapter "How to Be Yourself and Still Have Friends," the word "Friends" was misspelled. It said "Fiends." She looked it up in the dictionary to see if it was actually a word. It was. A fiend was an evil spirit or a wicked or cruel person. She thought that was very funny. "How to Be Yourself and Still Have Fiends."

There were three pages about getting your period. She didn't much care to read that part herself, and she knew if Toby found something like that in her room she'd have to move to Australia and start a new life. So she tore those pages right out of the book. It seemed wrong to throw them away, so she followed the thirty-four steps to open the Chinese puzzle box, folded the pages in half eight times, and placed them inside. "There, get inside and stay there, you *fiends,*" she declared, dropping the slats on both sides.

Taylor waited patiently for things to start happening, and sure enough one day they did. She was coming home from the library, turning the corner from Forty-first Avenue onto her own block, when her stomach did a major flip-flop. Rudy's blue Plymouth was parked out in front and he was inside it. She was going to have to pass right by him! He had his head back and his eyes shut so maybe he was asleep. But as she turned and started up the front sidewalk to her house he suddenly beeped the horn. She jumped and turned. He couldn't be beeping at her! Then Toby suddenly burst through the front door, bounding down the front steps in his big black boots.

"Chow," he said, flying past her.

"See ya," she replied, then turned a wistful face to watch as he opened the door and climbed in beside Rudy. She was embarrassed that she had imagined for a second that Rudy had been beeping at her, and quickly turned toward the house and began to plod up the wooden steps and across the landing. Toby was so lucky and he hardly knew it. Truth was, you just wanted to go somewhere on a day like this. You didn't want to be cooped up inside the house with nowhere to go and nothing to do.

"Hey!"

She pivoted, and was surprised to see Rudy's head hanging out the driver's side window. Was he talking to *her?*

"Hey, Taylor Finch! We're goin' for a ride," he shouted. "Want to come?"

Taylor shrugged and turned red. He was kidding. He was just teasing her, but that was okay. It was the most attention he'd ever paid her, and she liked it.

"Ruuuudy!" moaned her brother. "C'mon! Let's get going!"

But look at that Rudy, still hanging out the window.

"Hold on there, Tobe," he said. "Don't be in such a big hurry. Your sister might want to come with us for a change. Hey, Taylor? You can come if you want to. We're going over to the city."

Her mouth hung open, and she couldn't seem to close it. "Huh? What? Oh, no," she gasped, "I . . . I . . ." She pushed the hair out of her eyes and stood there on the porch landing looking down at them. She could not believe Rudy Garch was talking to her. It was exactly what she wanted to happen, a spectacular adventure to fill the whole afternoon stretching before her like a big empty chalkboard. Of course she wanted to go with them, but now she was scared.

"Just go on in the house," snapped Toby, jutting his head out the window, searing her with a steely eyed glare.

She shrunk a little inside but pretended not to hear him. It was surprisingly easy. But Rudy, was he serious or not? She couldn't tell from so far away.

She glanced at her brother's stony face and then quickly away. "All right, I'll come!" she blurted breathlessly, then tore down the front steps before Toby talked Rudy out of it or they forgot about her and drove off. As Toby climbed out of the car to let her into the backseat she avoided his squinty bullying scowl. She might pay for this later, but now it was fun.

"Try not to act stupid," he muttered, as she slid into the backseat. The old car shimmied and shuddered as he slammed the door, and she cringed. Yeah, she would pay for this later.

As they sped up Interstate 580 toward the San

Francisco Bay Bridge, Taylor had to pinch herself. Was she really going off with Rudy and her brother? She didn't even know where they were going or what they were doing, and she suddenly wished she'd left her mother a note. What would her mother think when she came home to find Taylor missing? She'd worry herself sick!

She glanced at the back of Rudy's head, then realized he was eyeing her in the rearview mirror. She blushed and turned to look out the window, twirling a strand of inky black hair around her finger.

"We're going to mess around in Chinatown," said Rudy. "That all right with you?"

"Mm hmm," she replied. She couldn't think of anything to say and felt stupid. She should've stayed home. She didn't want Toby to be mad at her for coming. She didn't want her mother to worry. She didn't want to make a fool of herself in front of Rudy. She'd just grabbed at the chance to do something different.

Now they were at the water and it was a pretty blue-gray. Rudy handed a dollar to the guy in the tollbooth and now they were rolling across the long span of the big Bay Bridge, higher and higher.

"There it is, San Francisco," said Rudy. "It's something, isn't it?"

Taylor looked off to her right, where a mighty army of buildings shimmered in the pale February sun. "Mm hmm," she said. "Wow!" She sat forward in her seat, straining to see everything because she hardly ever got to the city.

"Cat's got her tongue," said her brother.

"I don't have one and you know it," she replied. "A cat, I mean." Rudy chuckled but Toby didn't do anything. He seemed to be in a bad mood. She hoped it was not because of her, but she had a sneaking suspicion it might be. Maybe she ought to get out and take a bus back home once they crossed the bridge. Maybe she'd done the wrong thing in coming. She reached into her back pocket to make sure she had the ten dollars Toby had given her for her birthday. She carried it with her everywhere, just in case he changed his mind and snuck into her room to take it back. You never knew with Toby these days. She also liked the feel of money in her pocket. A ten-dollar bill seemed like a lot of money. It seemed like a lot more than just twice the amount of a five-dollar bill. Having ten dollars made her feel self-sufficient, as if she could take care of herself if ever she had to, and it might be right now.

The tall downtown buildings loomed so close—it was like seeing a movie or being in one. Her father had once taken her and Toby to the top of one of those buildings. She remembered how the ships in the bay had looked like toy boats. Those were the good old days, when her dad lived at home and Toby was different.

Toby leaned forward to turn on the radio. "Hey, that's a song from the tape you got for your birthday," he said, turning toward her.

It was nearly a nice thing to say and she smiled. "Yeah," she replied. "It's by RapSure. I like it."

Truth was, she didn't know how to take a bus back to Oakland and she didn't really want to.

Rudy cranked up the music and rolled down the windows. As the wind twirled long wisps of her hair around her face and head, she closed her eyes and imagined she was in a convertible up in the front seat next to Rudy. When she opened her eyes to find herself still in the backseat of the old Plymouth, she wasn't a bit disappointed. She was doing exactly what she wanted to be doing on this particular Saturday afternoon in February, and she began to snap her fingers to the music. She was twelve, and things really were changing.

Taylor stood with her face pressed to the glass, peering at a giant jar containing a big dead lizard immersed in some sort of fluid. There were also jars containing pickled pigs' feet and oxtails and dead snakes, which some Chinese used as medicine. But she couldn't take her eyes off the big dead lizard.

"Want one of those?"

It was Rudy, standing close behind her.

"Oh, no thank you!" she blurted, then covered her mouth to suppress a giggle. It was nervous laughter. If she started she might never stop.

Chinatown was like a foreign country. The narrow streets were jammed with people, mostly Chinese. There were Chinese bakeries, Chinese restaurants, Chinese gift shops, Chinese laundries and hardware stores, Chinese seafood markets, Chinese banks and libraries, and a Chinese McDonald's. Shop windows and menus were covered with Chinese writing.

Taylor followed Toby and Rudy up one crowded

street and down another, up this one and down that one. They were fast walkers, but she didn't have to worry about losing them. They were both tall. She could see their heads bobbing above most of the other people.

Once they turned down a narrow alley and ran smack into a fortune-cookie factory, with huge bags of fortune cookies stacked behind the window. A bag cost $4.50, but what would she do with a whole bag? If you ate ten cookies which fortune would you pay attention to? How would you know which one was right?

Now they were looking at a big oblong tub crammed with live catfish in the window of a small grocery store.

"How about that one?"

It was Rudy again, pointing to a fish, then giving her a little poke between her shoulder blades.

She smiled and shook her head, gazing at his reflection in the window. He was so cool and so much fun, but she kind of didn't know what to do. Here was this guy. He was sixteen years old and he was Toby's friend and he was paying her all this attention, and she liked it. When she got home she was going to write about it and hide it away in her secret box. She could hardly wait to do it, to see the words down on paper. She would write about the whole trip and how it was. She didn't know exactly how she would say it or what. She was just glad to have the secret box, and planned to keep it for the rest of her life. It had become that important.

Next to the tub of catfish there were three roasted ducks hanging by their feet from an iron bar, and big vats of chow mein and fried rice. The food looked delicious but she felt sorry for the catfish all crammed together and still sorrier after she saw the daily lunch special scrawled on a little blackboard: SAUTÉED CATFISH AND BROCCOLI WITH BLACK BEAN SAUCE AND RICE, $3.95.

She was glad they didn't eat there, but she was getting hungry. They soon found a Chinese bakery instead, and ordered little buns filled with pork and sausage and sweet bean paste, and a big pot of tea with three fortune cookies. They ate fast at a table in the corner and talked about cars—well, she didn't—and then Rudy was reading his fortune.

" 'Confucius say stuffed shirt is usually a very empty person.' I get it. Ha ha."

"Mine says 'Your dearest dish will come true,' " said Toby. "Oh, baby, I hope so." He gave his fortune a big kiss.

"Gimme that," said Rudy, snatching away the little paper fortune from his hand. "It says wish. 'Your dearest *wish* will come true.' Just as I thought, you big ham bone. Read yours, Taylor."

She suddenly felt tongue-tied again and terribly shy, her face going scarlet as she read. " 'You are wo-worrying about something that will never happen,' " she stammered, keeping her head down. She could feel Rudy's eyes right on her and she shrugged. She wanted to get up and run.

"That's a good one for you," said Toby. "The little worrier."

She felt her face get hot and red all over again. She

wanted to give him a good kick under the table, but he might kick her back. Later on she would think of some mean way to get back at him. She'd show him "little worrier," and someday soon!

"That's a stupid fortune," said Rudy. He shoved his chair back with a clatter, rose to his feet, and threw a few bills on the table. "I can do better than that myself. He who mashes potatoes shall not mash lips. There, how about that one? C'mon, let's blow this place."

She cupped her hand over her mouth and shrieked with laughter as she followed him out onto the street. "Oh, Rudy. . . ."

"Don't throw stone at glass house, lest little toe get chewed by big guard dog," blurted her brother.

It was pretty good too, and now she felt it was her turn but she didn't have one. "The thing you are worrying about is . . . is bound to happen," she mumbled, trailing a few feet behind. It was all she could think of.

Toby threw his head back and hooted, but Rudy turned and smiled. "That was pretty good, Taylor," he said. "You got the right idea."

Oh, he was nice. Nice wasn't really the right word. It didn't say anything. She would think of a better word later and write it down.

He slid his big arm around her shoulder, and now she was walking along right in between them. She wished she could see herself now, wished she were a little angel hovering just above them so she could see what she looked like walking down this busy Chinatown street in San Francisco with her brother and Rudy and Rudy's arm around her shoulder. She hardly dared breathe, lest it would end.

She figured they were headed for the car, but instead they entered a huge department store crammed with everything you could imagine: tea sets, fishing poles, fancy chopsticks, lamps and toys, pajamas and robes, pots and pans, ash trays, T-shirts, silver charms, CDs, telephones, and jewelry. You could shop for your whole family for Christmas for ten dollars.

She suddenly realized that Toby and Rudy had disappeared and she was standing in the middle of an aisle all alone. First she wandered around gazing at all the stuff. She had her ten dollars tucked away in her pocket, but she wasn't going to just spend it on anything. She saw some cool bracelets, and an expensive watch she wished she could get for her dad. Then she sorted through a pile of paper fans, thinking she would get one for her mother, who didn't like hot weather. She found one she thought her mom would like, white with pink and green flowers. It was only $2.50 and she almost decided to get it.

Then she discovered a whole row of earring racks and hardly knew where to look first. She spun one of the display racks around and around, then chose a pair of small cat-face earrings to try on. Cute! And she could get them if she wanted to.

"Hey, those are really cool."

It was Rudy, of course. She saw his reflection in the mirror. That nice smile and his smooth jaw and the jacket collar up around his neck.

"I might buy them," she said proudly. "I've got ten dollars of my own."

"Yeah? Cool. Hey, you should hang onto your money. How about if I get them for you?" He snatched them from her before she could say a thing and disappeared around the corner.

Once again, she didn't know what to do. Chase after him and say no thank you? Why would she want to do that? She shoved her empty hand into her pocket and slipped around the corner herself. He was gone, vanished. Should she wait for him here? Did he really like her and was he buying her those earrings?

She strolled toward the front of the store, keeping an eye out for Toby and Rudy. There they were, waiting outside, and her brother looked hopping mad.

"What kept you?" he snapped, as she slipped through the front door. "Can't you see you're holding us up!"

Tears sprung to her eyes and she rushed to brush them away. She didn't know why he was so mad. Rudy'd just left her two minutes ago.

The two guys took off like a couple of wild horses. She stared angrily at the back of her brother's head as she ran to keep up with them. Let them race away and leave her if they wanted to. She had ten dollars and could get home on her own.

When they stopped for a red light at the end of the block, Rudy stopped and turned to look at her. "Don't pay attention to this knucklehead!" he said, grinning. He grabbed Toby by the collar and rapped him twice on the head. "He's just a wise guy."

Wrestling himself out of Rudy's grip, Toby laughed and so did she. Everything was all right again. Maybe her fortune was right too, and there was nothing at all to worry about.

After crossing the street they went halfway up the next block, turned down an alley, then wound back toward the car by way of a couple of side streets.

"Hey, we made it," said Rudy, digging his car keys from his back pocket.

"Yeah," gasped Taylor, too out of breath from walking uphill to say anything more. She had a million thoughts tumbling through her mind, though, and feelings, too.

"Hey, I got something for you, remember?" said Rudy. He smiled.

Of course she remembered. She swept her hair out of her eyes and shyly studied the ground as he stuck his hand inside his jacket and pulled out the little cat earrings.

"Oh!" she exclaimed, and then "Oh!" again, as a sudden cascade of objects from inside his jacket spilled to the ground. She stood gawking at the heap of stuff at his feet: an expensive watch from that store they were in, a pocket calculator, two CDs and a cordless phone!

"You dropped something," said Toby, jeering from the other side of the car.

"What's all this . . . ?" She took a step toward Rudy and stopped. "Oh . . . oh . . ." she stammered. "I guess . . ." She looked to her brother for some sort of sign, something to make her think that what she thought was happening wasn't really.

"Maybe you should give her the phone." Toby sneered. "Then she can call you at San Quentin from the privacy of her own room."

Rudy laughed as he stooped to pick up the stuff. They were all laughing now, she right along with them, even though her heart had just sunk all the way to her toes. She just didn't know what else to do.

"People who own stores are rich," explained Rudy, glancing up at her as he slipped the CDs back into his jacket. "This is peanuts to them. They don't miss a couple things like this. If they did they'd all be out of business."

She nodded, and clutching the little cat earrings, squeezed herself into the backseat of the old blue Plymouth. All the way home, she could hear her brother playing with all the gadgets on his new Swiss army knife. ". . . scissors . . . screwdriver . . . can opener . . . pliers . . . big knife . . . little knife . . . nail file . . . tweezers . . . saw . . ."

She was no dummy. She'd be calling them both in San Quentin.

"Where have you *been?*"

Her mother was mad. 'Course she was mad, and worried, too. "It's not like you, Taylor!" said her mom. "What in the world made you think you could go off without asking permission?" Taylor did not have a good answer, or any answer, so she cocked her head to one side and lifted her shoulders in a shrug.

"And where is your brother?"

"He went off with Rudy," Taylor replied hoarsely, her arms hanging at her sides like two heavy ropes.

She didn't feel bad about being sent to her room. In fact, she was glad. She raced up the stairs, down the short hallway, and pulled the door to her bedroom shut behind her. Then she sat slumped and shivering on the edge of her bed, her hands balled up and stuffed into the pockets of her sweatshirt. She was afraid to take them out, because of what was in them.

She wanted to remember how the day was before Rudy gave her the earrings. She just wanted to have the memory of walking down the streets of Chinatown with Rudy and her brother, Rudy's arm on her shoulder. Of eating the little Chinese buns, making up fortunes, riding in the backseat of Rudy's old car as it sailed across the bridge over all that blue water.

Her lower lip quivered as she pulled her left hand from her pocket and slowly opened it. She wished it weren't so, but the cat earrings were still there, still pinned to the small square of cardboard. Was she a thief, too? She dropped them onto the bed, then tried to rub away the imprint of the cat earrings in the palm of her hand, but it wouldn't go away.

The day felt ruined. Her wonderful time with Rudy all ruined. She grabbed the earrings and threw them into the wastebasket. There!

But Rudy Garch gave them to you, a voice inside her said. He gave them to *you,* so you can't throw them away. She leaned forward and plucked the earrings from the wastebasket, holding them in her clenched hand as she stood unmoving in the middle of the room.

Rudy had taken them, but now they were hers!

Rudy had given them to her because he liked her! She didn't steal them! You shouldn't throw away something somebody gave you. He might want her to wear them one day, if he . . . if they . . . went out . . . someday when she was older, maybe. . . .

She reached for the Chinese puzzle box on her dresser. First her hands flew through the thirty-four steps as never before, then she shoved the earrings inside and slapped the cover back on. Presto! Done deal! The problem was solved. Now they wouldn't be right in her face. Now she could look at them once in a while and remember who gave them to her. And if she forgot about them for a while, she might even come to forget they were stolen. And then she could actually wear them. Earrings, from Rudy Garch!

Sometimes Taylor Finch did forget about the earrings she got from Rudy Garch. But whenever she thought of something she wanted to hide away in her secret box, then she remembered them. Also, whenever she opened the box she saw not only the little cat faces smiling up at her, but also the expensive watch and the CDs and the cordless phone and Toby flipping the blades on the red Swiss army knife in the front seat of the old blue Plymouth. She didn't want to see those things— they were all stolen. So she'd drop the lid on the secret box and try to think of some other place to hide things. It was kind of making her mad. It didn't feel like her box anymore. And what good was a secret box if you couldn't use it?

When she and her friends Deirdre and Robin wrote a secret communication code, she had to slip the sheet of paper under her mattress instead. Then there was the ring that belonged to her grandmother, which now was hers. It belonged in a very special place and where better than the secret box. But no, she had to put it in her old jewelry box instead, along with the rest of her stuff.

It was all churning around inside her, bound to eventually come to a head, and one hot day at the end of May it did. She'd gone to the store for her mother and was on her way out, walking through the automatic exit with her nose half buried in the bag of groceries. Oh, how she loved the smell of fresh bread. It was hard not to start in on it right away. She lifted her head, saw a big red-and-black sign posted in the front window of the Stop 'n' Shop Supermarket, and came to a dead stop.

SHOPLIFTERS WILL BE PROSECUTED TO THE FULLEST EXTENT OF THE LAW.

She stood there for a full minute, rereading the sign. What did that mean, "the fullest extent of the law"? "The fullest extent of the law," she repeated, moving her lips. It sounded bad. It sounded terrible, and she hurried toward home with her head tucked over the bag of groceries. "I am not a shoplifter," she mumbled to herself as she went. "I am not a thief. I just happened to be there."

She felt it was really true for a block or two—she knew deep down she was not a thief—and then the doubts came back, scurrying about in her mind. Was she or wasn't she? She wanted to get home so she could write the words down— "I am not a thief"—and always remember them. She would write them down before she even had a piece of fresh bread, and then she would lock what she wrote away in her secret box and never forget it. That twelve-year-old girl in her class had gone to juvie for stealing or something, but she would not be going to juvie because she hadn't stolen anything.

She walked faster and faster, and when she got to her own block she saw Rudy's car parked out in front of her house. He was not in it.

Clutching the bag of groceries to her chest, Taylor came to a standstill in the middle of the sidewalk. Her heart began to pound in the old familiar way. Where was Rudy? Was he inside the house? Was he off somewhere with Toby? She stood gawking at his car for another minute and then she began to run. First the bread flew from the bag onto the sidewalk and she stopped to retrieve it. Then a package of table napkins erupted and she had to pick that up too. But she kept on going.

She pounded up the front steps—Rudy nowhere in sight—through the front door, across the living room, and up the twelve stairs to her bedroom. She dumped the bag of groceries onto her bed, grabbed the Chinese puzzle box from the top of her dresser, and opened it as fast as she could.

She yanked the cat earrings from the box, then plucked them from the cardboard square they were pinned to. She was wearing a gold stud in each ear; she removed them, replacing each one with a cat earring.

When all that was done, she raced back downstairs and out the front door.

Whew! No Rudy in sight. That was sure lucky. She sat down on the front steps to wait. It was hot. Soon the heat from the wooden porch steps was broiling her butt and the sun was scorching her face. She moved into a strip of shade and, cupping her hands over her eyes, scoured the streets for some sign of Rudy.

A half hour went by. Other people passed by in cars and on foot. Drops of sweat ran down her back and trickled down the bridge of her nose. Her sliver of shade was about to disappear and still she sat waiting. Rudy Garch.

Way way down the block she could see someone coming, somebody tall. She scooted forward and sat up taller. Could it be him? She fingered the earring in her left ear and then the earring in her right ear, and wriggled her frosted toes in her sandals.

Yes, she knew that walk. It was him. And she was wearing the earrings he had given to her. What would he think? Would he like them? Would he say anything about them?

She could see two people coming. Was the other person her brother? If he and Rudy went somewhere, would they ask her to go with them? And if they did? . . .

She frowned slightly and looked away. If they did ask her . . . She closed her eyes and gulped some air. She could see herself up in the front seat of Rudy's car, Rudy with his arm around her shoulder. The radio was blaring. Toby smiled and said something nice. He was in the backseat and he was holding something in his hand. What was it?

She opened her eyes and turned her head toward the two beanpoles swaggering toward her down the hot white sidewalk. It was Rudy okay, looking as usual like he owned half the world, but the guy next to him . . . he was awful tough looking. . . . It wasn't her . . . She squinted and jutted her head forward, as though a few inches would make a big difference. Was it her brother or not?

If it was and they asked her to go somewhere and they went into some store . . . She swallowed. She didn't want to think about those things but she couldn't help it.

She closed her eyes because she wanted to see Rudy Garch with his arm on her shoulder. She could hear him laughing, saying, You want this? You want that?

It was Toby all right. It was her brother looking tough like that, hunched forward scowling, hands buried deep in his pockets, and maybe in one of those pockets he carried the Swiss army knife he'd stolen that day in Chinatown.

She was not a thief, and if they asked her to go . . .

She closed her eyes and tried to hear Toby say something nice. But she couldn't. She kept them closed and tried again. Then all the hurt and disappointment inside her rushed up to where she could feel it. She brushed away the tears that sprang to her eyes, and rose to her feet. Pulling the cat earrings free, she descended the steps with her head down and crossed the front lawn. When she reached Rudy's blue Plymouth, she tossed the earrings into the backseat and turned to go.

"I am not a thief," she murmured to herself as she strode back across the lawn to the house and up the front steps. "But I am related to one." She rubbed the tears from her cheeks, and let the screen door bang shut behind her.

Cousin Dolores

The Phone Call

She couldn't see him, but she could hear the *tap tap swish,* indicating that her brother Eric (she called him "Eric de Merit") was still shooting baskets in the driveway. The driveway ran along the side of the house, but the sound of the ball hitting the pavement carried well. It seemed to echo inside her head. *Tap tap swish. Tap tap klunk* when he missed and the ball hit the backboard. It was annoying. It spoiled her concentration, which wasn't much to begin with when it came to word problems. She scowled at the open book on the kitchen table and scooted her numb butt forward on her chair.

If Berniece's Boogie Burger uses a quarter pound of potatoes for one regular order of french fries, and a third of a pound of potatoes for *(tap tap klunk)* a large order of french fries, how many pounds of potatoes will it take *(tap tap)* to serve the twenty-one members *(swish)* of the Ripperton County Dog and Doughnut Club, who order seven large orders *(tap)* of fries and *(tap)* eleven regular orders of *(klunk)* fries?

She absentmindedly rotated the eraser end of her pencil into her lower lip until it began to burn. Her mother said it was a bad habit. Eric said it was how moles that appeared later in life first got their start. She stopped rotating the pencil, because she did not want a mole on her lip in later life, and tapped her cheek with the pencil instead.

Out of the corner of her eye she spied the saltine crackers stacked beside her on the kitchen table. She used them as rewards because she loved them. Finish a problem—pop a buttered cracker into her mouth. If they were out of saltines, she used graham crackers, but her mom wouldn't permit her an endless supply of those because they contained more sugar. She liked to remind her mother that Grandma Betty had often made Lindsey sugar sandwiches—white bread spread with butter and sugar—and nothing bad had happened. To her anyway. Her grandma had passed away the previous year, but Lindsey didn't think it was because of sugar sandwiches. It was old age or a run-down heart.

. . . a quarter pound of potatoes for one regular order of french fries . . . She wanted a cracker, and she wanted it now, and a curse on all those mean people who created these ridiculous problems, these instruments of torture!

Removing a saltine from the top of the stack, she popped it into her mouth and read on. Each problem was harder than the one before, and she was only on number three out of ten!

She bit her lip in frustration, trying to hold back a tear. Give me a science experiment, she thought to herself. I can handle that. Give me an essay to write, give me a poem to memorize, give me a picture to paint, a geography lesson, a history lesson . . . the rings in P.E. (Which she hated. They made her nauseous. The last thing she ever wanted to be was a gymnast. She didn't like to fling her body about in weird contortions. And those "horses"! Why did they call them horses and how insulting! And bouncing sky-high on the trampoline until your insides had turned to mush, until your organs had all switched places, including your heart, which was now in your mouth, of course. Just give her a volleyball, a softball, a tennis ball. Let the ball hurl out of control through space—not her!)

She flung down her pencil in disgust and frustration. It bounced off the table and scattered clear across the kitchen floor. Yes, she did hate these word problems.

Tap tap tap tap tap tap tap swish.

She jumped to her feet and shoved the kitchen window up over her head. "Stop it!" she screamed, poking her head out. "I'm trying to do my homework!" She slammed the window shut and sat back down.

Truth was, she didn't feel like she was too good at anything these days, and it was affecting her nerves.

Brrrrrrnnnnng.

She jumped several inches off the chair. Then her mother's hand appeared around the corner, lifting the phone from its cradle.

"Oh, hi, Flo," said her mother, Ellen.

Flo was Lindsey's aunt, married to her uncle Mo. They were rich and lived in the hills of Piedmont, overlooking the cities of Oakland and Berkeley.

"What's *wrong*, Flo?" Lindsey's mother, now standing in the kitchen, was frowning. "What's happened?"

Lindsey made a quick study of her mother's face. Not Uncle Mo, she said to herself. Please, not Uncle Mo.

"Oh, no. Oh, *no*," cried Ellen. "Oh, Flo, I'm so sorry."

"What?" Lindsey mouthed to her mother. "What's wrong?"

Her mother shook her head, but what did that mean? Don't worry? Don't bother me? No *what?* Lindsey was sure something had happened to her uncle. He'd driven his small red sports car off a cliff. He'd been caught in an avalanche up in the Sierra Nevada. Uncle Mo had a lot of close calls but always lived to tell a good story. Maybe not this time.

"When did it happen?" asked her mother. She glanced at Lindsey and slowly shook her head, the way parents do when they're about to say, "What a shame."

"What a shame. And so close to home. Poor Mo, poor Mo. I'm so sorry, Flo."

Lindsey began to feel sick to her stomach. Poor Aunt Flo. What would she do without Uncle Mo?

"I just hope it was painless," sighed Ellen.

What? Lindsey mouthed again to her mother, but her mother gave no sign of recognition.

"Now, Flo, what can we do to help? You just name it. Anything at all . . ."

Lindsey slumped forward, cradling her head in her arms. She'd work on word problems every day until she was fifty if it would only bring her uncle back from the dead.

Her lips brushed against a crumb on the table and she lifted her head in revulsion. Ick. She was sure it was something left behind by inconsiderate Eric de Merit, and she flicked it away with her finger.

"On Sunday—what can we bring? Sure, let us know later. We'll be thinking about you, and we'll be sure to say a special prayer."

Lindsey heard the phone clink softly into the receiver, signaling an impending announcement. Even with her head down on the table, Lindsey could see her uncle's face as plain as if he were standing in front of her. It was big and round and pinkish, like a grapefruit.

"I've got bad news," said her mother.

"I *know*," said Lindsey, lifting her head. "What *is* it?"

"Dolores was hit by a car."

Lindsey's jaw dropped. "Dolores?" she repeated. "Hit by a car?"

"Yeah, early this afternoon. Poor Dolores. When she didn't come home for her nap, Mo drove around the neighborhood looking for her. He found her lying beside a curb a few blocks away. Poor Mo."

Yes, poor Uncle Mo, thought Lindsey, but he was a *lot*

better off than he'd been a few moments ago in her mind. She was now faced with an awkward set of feelings. She was so relieved to hear that Uncle Mo wasn't dead she could've done a little dance around the kitchen, hardly appropriate under the circumstances.

"Gee, I can't believe it," she murmured. "Poor Dolores."

"Naturally, Flo is awfully upset, crying and everything." Shaking her head, Lindsey's mother crossed the room and sat down. "I don't think Dolores suffered much, honey. That kind of a thing happens so fast, you know. Boom, and they're gone."

Lindsey nodded, hoping her mother was right. Now it was starting to sink in—Dolores was really gone. Hit by a car. Her homely head now appeared in Lindsey's mind, the long, wet snout and stiff, pointy ears, the eyes shiny and bulgy in their sockets like little black bulbs. That scraggly, misshapen body. Dolores was not an attractive animal but Mo and Flo loved her like a daughter. She'd had, in fact, her own carpeted bedroom, a color TV, a twin bed with a Sealy Posturepedic mattress and pink doggie blanket, and a toy box loaded with dozens of chewed-up things.

"It's almost like losing a cousin," said Lindsey, turning a wistful face up to her mother. She had actually preferred the company of Dolores to some of her real cousins, who perhaps were better looking but too obnoxious or too silly or too boring. "Cousin Dolores," she repeated. "And now she's gone."

★　　★　　★

After her mother left the kitchen, Lindsey gazed glumly out the window into the yard, where the cherry blossom tree had suddenly sprung to life in all its pink glory. Spring was around the corner, and Dolores wouldn't be here to see it. Lindsey tried to imagine never seeing Dolores again *(tap)* but she couldn't. Death was *(tap)* too hard to understand, too *(klunk)* final.

She returned her gaze to her open math book, suddenly wondering if her uncle's life had been spared because she'd committed herself to word problems for the next thirty-seven years. It seemed neither fair nor likely, so she *(tap)* closed the book *(klunk)*.

Halfway down the hall she passed Eric on his way to the shower.

"Cousin Dolores is dead!" she blurted. "Not that you'd give a hoot!"

He stood there dripping sweat, his mouth a surprised little hoop. She knew he was about to say "Cousin who?" but she didn't give him a chance. Why bother? She bounded past him straight for her room and shut the door.

Eric de Merit

The house was a whirl of activity and it wasn't helping Lindsey's nerves. Her mother was doing the laundry down at the end of the hall. Her father was frying meatballs in the kitchen. Her adopted brother, Tu, was playing the drums in his room.

Lindsey held the tangled ball of wire at arm's length and shook her head. She was off to a bad start. She'd once seen a fisherman snag his line on something like this. It was frightful. She was trying not to feel discouraged, but it certainly didn't look like a work of art so far, not to mention a good representation of Cousin Dolores. She picked up the wire cutter and snipped off the curlicue tail. Perhaps then it would look more like a dog than a pig. Then she grabbed another hanger from the dwindling pile on the living-room floor, and, using a pliers, began to unwind it.

She was creating a work of art to present to Aunt Flo and Uncle Mo at Dolores's funeral the next day, Sunday. It was going to be a life-sized sculpture of Dolores, something they could keep in honor of her memory. The idea had come to her yesterday, Friday, while sitting in her fifth period art class, taught by the red-haired Mr. Peek, whom she liked very much. He once told her she had "natural talent." Ever since then she'd been trying to prove it and not done as well.

Her brainstorm had actually been in incubation that whole day, a day in which everybody she knew seemed to have a story about pets they had lost: little green turtles squished in that small space between the bottom of the screen door and the floor; sleepy-eyed chameleons slithering off into wall cracks, never to be seen or heard from again; goldfish exploding in the middle of the night; and rabbits appearing as entrées at posh neighborhood restaurants.

The loss of a chameleon didn't seem like much in comparison to a dog like Dolores. You didn't hear people say, "Oh, how I miss my chameleon," when they went on vacation. And you couldn't tell if a chameleon liked you or not. Well, Dolores had really liked *her*, Lindsey, and she had liked Dolores, and this was the least she could do. Besides, her other sculpture project hadn't been going that well.

As Lindsey tugged and yanked at a particularly stubborn wire hanger, the sweat began to pool on her forehead. She wiped her face with the sleeve of her sweatshirt, trying to remember what Mr. Peek had said about sculpting. It didn't really matter. This was not sculpting. This was wrestling, and she knew that he would not approve of her method. He would tell her not to force things, to "listen to the materials you are using, let them speak to you, mold and shape with your heart as well as your hands." She did not think that the coat hanger was about to speak to her, and if it did she might give up sculpting that very minute. Instead, she spoke to the coat hanger.

"Oh, drat you!"

But it wasn't the coat hanger's fault. It was her fault for preferring heavy hangers to the wimpy kind that collapsed under the weight of a single pair of jeans. Mr. Peek had given them each a small spool of aluminum wire to create a sculpture with, but she had needed more for Cousin Dolores. She hadn't known *what* she was going to use, until she pulled a shirt off a hanger that morning and—presto!—there was the answer. Of course, her room looked like a junk heap now, with clothes from the closet dumped onto her bed, but so what?

"Watcha working on?"

It was Eric. He stood slouching against the doorjamb in his baggy blue sweats, ready to bother her.

"An art project." She shrugged. He ought to see that she was busy and unavailable for conversation.

"Let me guess," he said, yawning, heading her way. "It's . . ."

"No. Don't come near me."

"Why not?" He got halfway across the living room and stopped.

"What's wrong with you!" cried Lindsey. "Can't you see that I'm busy!"

"I was just . . ."

"Just going to bother me. Obviously, you can't *tell* what it is yet, and I don't want to play guessing games. I just started, and I've got to keep working."

"It's for Peek's class, right? I made something like that once. Want a few pointers?"

She grabbed the wire cutter and thrust it menacingly toward him. "No. Would you?"

"Okay, okay." He held up his hands in mock defeat, then backed his way out of the room.

"Pest," she muttered, under her breath. Her friend Taylor Finch was lucky. Her brother left her alone. She wished Eric would leave her alone too, get himself a girlfriend or something. But what girl would want him? She didn't!

Was Dolores's nose too long or too short? It was hard to tell, and hard having a goofball for a brother, instead of somebody she could look up to.

Beads of sweat gathered like little dewdrops on her forehead as she used a pliers to untwist another coat hanger. Then she rose to her feet, planting a foot on one end of the coat hanger and pulling on the other end in order to straighten it. She'd had no idea art could be such hard work. But it would all be worth it when she presented it to her aunt and uncle.

She tried to recall the exact shape of poor Dolores's body as she worked. Dolores's legs were about as thick as the legs on the coffee table right here in front of her. If she wrapped the coat hanger around a coffee table leg she might get the shape just right, but she could scratch the table. Her own arm was bigger, but if she wound the wire tightly around it, it just might work.

As an artist you had to be clever! You had to keep thinking!

She held her left arm up in front of her and considered the possibility. Yes, it was a good idea. She smiled as she began to wrap the coat hanger around her left arm, pleased with herself indeed.

"Hey, now what're you doing?"

Lindsey started and lifted her head. He was back.

"Obviously still working," she replied curtly, tucking her left arm behind her.

"But what's that on your arm?"

"What are you talking about? You know, Eric, you annoy the heck out of me. You really do. You just stand there with this smirk on your face when I'm trying to really accomplish something here. Tomorrow is Dolores's funeral and Uncle Mo and Aunt Flo are feeling just awful. . . ."

"I know! It's a little casket!"

She felt a catch in her throat. How could he say such a thing?

"Is that supposed to be funny?" she said, swallowing. "Always the jokester, Mr. de Merit. Always the jokester. I'm trying to do something . . . to . . . to make a contribution, and all you do is bother people. I don't even think you care that Dolores is dead!" she cried, swatting the floor with her hand.

"Sure I do," he said calmly. "She was a good dog, but . . ." He shrugged.

"But what?" she cried. "But what? She was too what? Too ugly. Is that it? She wasn't cute enough for you? Is that it? She was just a dog, you know, Eric. She wasn't running for Miss America. She wasn't up for Homecoming Queen. She was just a dog, a simple dog with . . . who . . ."

And then he did that thing, that thing she hated so much. He folded his arms, arched his left eyebrow, and glared right at her. It was his "evil eye" and he did it to make her laugh, especially when she did not feel like laughing. But she would not laugh. Not this time.

"I'm really worried about you," she replied through clenched teeth. "You don't care about anyone or anything. You always have to be funny. Perhaps you're a little insane." She forgot about her arm in its wire contraption and swung it around in front of her.

"Perhaps," he said drily, eyeing her arm with a smirk. "It does tend to run in the family."

She looked around for something to throw at him. A book from the table, a chair . . . A chair might kill him. Was that really necessary?

★   ★   ★

Her arm was beginning to throb. She tried to slip the contraption down over her hand, but the end of the wire had snagged on the rolled-up sleeve of her shirt. It was a new shirt and she didn't want to tear it. She moved from the floor up to the sofa. What should she do now?

She looked down at her arm in its little coat hanger sling. She felt sorry for her arm and sorry for Dolores. It was going to be hard to go to her funeral. Lindsey hated funerals. The last funeral she'd been to was her grandmother's. Everybody was crying. It was awful crying in public, awful seeing your parents and all your relatives cry. She tried to remember if Eric had cried. She didn't think so.

Lindsey glanced at her left hand with some alarm. It was turning blue. Just then the doorbell rang and she got up to answer it. It was Taylor Finch from across the street.

"Hi," said Taylor. "Can you go to a movie?"

"Hi," said Lindsey. "No, I can't. I'm working on something."

"Hey, what's that on your arm? Are you being punished?"

Lindsey looked at her arm, stiff and straight in its coat-hanger cage. "No. It's my art project."

"Oh, like a bracelet," said Taylor. "Cool."

"It's an armlet."

"An *omelet?*"

"No, an *arm*let."

"Cool," said Taylor. "How'd you do that?"

"Tell you later," said Lindsey. "I've got to finish my project."

She shut the door, then paused in the hall between the living room and the kitchen to examine her hand. It looked like a dead fish. How could she work with one hand?

The Swamp Doggie

By the time her parents removed the hanger from Lindsey's arm her hand had turned the same shade of blue as a popular brand of mouthwash. They suggested she be more careful, and gently waggle her arm about until the numbness was gone. So she went to the movies with Taylor, who by that time was wearing an armlet of her own.

After the movie Lindsey secluded herself in her room and went back to work on the sculpture. She felt rather inspired with both hands free again and soon worked herself into a frenzy. Eventually her closet was empty but Dolores was as big as a cow.

"Big as a cow, bow wow," she said to herself, laughing.

She created Dolores's legs by wrapping hangers around broom handles, then scoured the house for just the right object for Dolores's torso, happily settling on the Hoover upright vacuum cleaner.

She finished the sculpture around ten thirty that night, studying it for several minutes from across the room, as you were supposed to do with real works of art. She was ecstatic. She was euphoric. It was good! It was great! It was . . . big! It looked . . . well, a lot like Dolores! Surely she would get an A from the red-haired Mr. Peek, who perhaps would become her mentor and tell future biographers how she'd stumbled upon her career path at the humble age of thirteen.

She wondered where her aunt and uncle would put it. Would they hang it from the ceiling, or place it upon a pedestal in their big formal living room? She was exhausted and ready to drop into bed, but her bed was buried under a monstrous heap of clothing. How would she find something to wear to church in the morning, and Dolores's funeral after that? She hauled her sleeping bag down from the closet shelf, threw it across the bedroom floor, and fell asleep instantly.

When she awoke the next morning, it was early and not quite light, and her hip was sore from sleeping on the wood floor. She rolled over yawning, wondering what she was doing on the floor in the first place, and slowly opened her eyes.

"Aaaaah!" She let out a yelp and grabbed her pillow in the event the intruder chose to attack. But everything came back to her in a matter of seconds.

She threw the pillow down and gaped at the monster. Easing herself up onto her knees, she let out a low moan. It did not look like Dolores at all. It did look like something prehistoric, something that might have crawled out of the sludge of some cesspool and gone about eating its young. "Swamp doggie," she muttered, dropping her chin to her knees. She'd created a monster, a hideous piece of junk, and she pictured the red-haired Mr. Peek throwing his head back and howling. He would describe it to all the other teachers in the teachers' lounge, and they would all throw their heads back and howl.

She threw on a pair of jeans and a sweatshirt and began to slide Dolores carefully across the floor toward her bedroom door. She'd slide it down the hallway, through the kitchen, and out the back door, then carry it out to the garage before anyone else was up. She could figure out what to do with it later.

She slid it right up to the door, then scowled deeply with dismay. Dolores *was* as big as a cow, a cow that couldn't get through the doorway. Lindsey tried every angle but the thing was just too big. Big as a cow, bow wow. Now she could hear somebody up making coffee and somebody bringing in the paper. She closed her bedroom door and scooted Dolores back into a corner. So much for an A from Mr. Peek. So much for a keepsake for her aunt and uncle. With a loud sigh of frustration and disappointment, she flung a blanket over Dolores's head. She'd have to squash it and bury it later. Same fate as the real dog.

A Solemn Occasion

Her eyes were like slits in her head. She hadn't slept well on the floor, and hadn't slept long enough. Periodically, her head fell forward onto her chest. After a moment or two, assaulted by a stinky mustard smell from the bowl of potato salad in her lap, her head snapped back into an upright position.

"What's it like to get buried?" asked Tu. He was sitting between her and Eric in the backseat of their car on the way to Dolores's funeral.

"It's ... it's ... well ...," stammered her mother from the front seat. "It's ... it's just like being an acorn."

Lindsey's head rolled about on her neck like a giant top, like a little globe on its axis. Had her mother actually said that, or had she dreamed it? An *acorn?* She'd never heard anything so ridiculous in her life, and it creeped her out. *Really* creeped her out. To live a full, happy and productive life, then imagine eternity as an ... *acorn?* It wasn't a good answer, and she could feel Tu fidgeting beside her.

"Look at all these fancy cars," noted her father from behind the wheel, as he headed the car up Mo and Flo's circular drive toward the front of their big gold and green stucco mansion. "It looks like a send-off for some big-politico. Maybe we should've brought caviar instead of meatballs and potato salad."

"What's caviar?" asked Tu.

"Fish eggs," said Eric. "You eat them."

"*You* eat them," said Tu in a little outburst. *Buried like an acorn.* He was also obviously outraged.

"It's not normal," said Eric. "Doing this sort of thing for a dog. I hope we eat soon."

"This is a solemn occasion," said Lindsey, rubbing her eyes. "Try to think of something besides your stomach. And when we do eat, try to keep your food where it belongs. Their carpet's worth about twenty thousand big buckeroos."

Her father whistled. "How do you know that?"

"Auntie Flo told me."

"What's normal?" said Tu.

"Normal is what most people are like," Lindsey explained very carefully.

"Am I normal?" asked Tu.

"Yes," she replied, smiling. "You are."

"Is Dad normal?"

"Yes, Dad is normal."

"Are you normal?"

She should not have hesitated. It gave them time to consider, and now they were laughing—at her expense. She tried to smile, to show that she knew it was a joke, but her face mirrored in the car window showed someone more perturbed than amused.

She suddenly felt sick to her stomach. Maybe it was the lack of sleep or her father's driving. Maybe it was the smell of mustard or the thought of being buried like an acorn. She heaved her shoulder against the car door, popping it open and poking her legs out.

"I *am* normal," she declared to anyone who cared to listen. "Just as normal as any of the rest of you." But as she lugged the bowl of potato salad across the front lawn and up the twenty-six steps to her aunt and uncle's front door, she had a sudden vision of that monstrous contraption hidden under a sleeping bag in her bedroom. That monster *she* had created.

Aunt Flo answered the door. Lindsey nearly burst into tears. "Oh, Auntie," she murmured. "I'm sorry. . . ."

Aunt Flo extended her arms and pulled Lindsey close. "Thank you, Lindsey. It's hard to believe, isn't it? Here one minute and gone the next. Just like that. Dolores really loved you, you know, just like I do."

The bowl of potato salad, thrust uncomfortably into Lindsey's belly, nearly knocked the wind right out of her. She took a deep breath but got a big whiff of her aunt's syrupy-sweet perfume. When she came up for air, she was face-to-face with a panting black dog the size of Smokey the Bear.

"Down, Jupiter, down!" cried her aunt. "Rein him in, Frieda, before he bowls us over! You go ahead and find yourself a seat," she said to Lindsey, "and I'll take this lovely salad to the table."

Lindsey did not want to sit near her family. We'll see who's normal, she thought, still stung by the insinuations made in the car. She found herself a seat on the sofa beside a woman who introduced herself as Mrs. Green. Then Mrs. Green introduced her dog, Tuesday, a fidgety ball of fur in a little red sweater. Aunt Flo returned to the living room shortly thereafter, introducing Mr. Birdsong and his bulldog, Dawn Marie; a Mrs. Frieda Philpott and her big dog, Jupiter; and Aunt Flo's brother, Roger Knipe, who'd brought his bagpipes instead of a dog.

Where was Uncle Mo? Lindsey wondered. Oh, there, perched on a small wooden chair in a far corner of the living room, rolling the end of a cigar roughly the size of a small cucumber around and around in his mouth. He didn't look to Lindsey as if he'd just lost a beloved dog or a beloved anything. Except maybe his lighter.

"Thank you all for coming," said Flo, seated on a folding chair between Lindsey's parents. "Dolores would have been so pleased. As you know, she was a special dog, and beloved by us. We had her for thirteen years and loved her like a child."

Seeing her aunt's eyes well with tears, Lindsey felt a catch in the back of her throat and swallowed. Frieda Philpott had also been weeping. Her face was a mottled pinkish gray, a color Lindsey had only seen before in Play-Doh. Every time Frieda wiped her nose, her dog, Jupiter, gagged. This was because she'd wrapped both a handkerchief and Jupiter's leash around the same two fingers on her right hand. Wipe her nose—yank the leash. It was pathetic, really.

"We thought we'd spend a few moments remembering Dolores," said Flo. "If you have something you'd like to say, just go ahead and share it."

"I guess I'll start," said Frieda Philpott. "Dolores was a wonderful dog and a fantastic playmate for Jupiter. We still can't believe she's really gone, can we, Jupey? We knew her for thirteen years, and we'll miss her dearly, won't we, Jupey?" She raised the handkerchief to swipe at her nose. Jupiter lurched forward, gagging, a long string of drool swinging from his mouth.

If Mrs. Philpott weren't careful, thought Lindsey, there'd be another funeral to go to. She yawned, covering her mouth with the back of her hand.

"Thank you, Frieda," said Flo. "Thank you so much." She left the room and quickly returned with an empty pie tin, which she placed directly under Jupiter's long pink tongue. "I hope you don't mind," she whispered discreetly. "It's just . . . you know . . . the carpet. . . ."

"I remember Dolores as a puppy," declared Mrs.

Green. "My, my, she was a *cuuuuuuu*tie. She'd sneak into our yard to play with our first dog, Sunday, before Sunday passed on. And, oh! How she loved hamburgers hot off the grill. We never had a barbecue without Dolores dropping by." Mrs. Green sighed and shook her head. At her feet, Tuesday yapped sharply.

Lindsey's throat felt marbley and weird and her eyes were beginning to smart. All these people remembering Dolores. It was a solemn occasion indeed. She lowered her head and folded her hands. She was not going to cry in front of everyone.

Now Mr. Birdsong was speaking. He had a very deep voice, an attribute his name did nothing to imply.

"Dawn Marie and Dolores both went to Billy Foster's Dog Camp together last summer," he boomed.

Lindsey heard someone sniffle but kept her head down. Dawn Marie panted on the floor beside Mr. Birdsong. With her enormous drooping jowls, she looked more like a "Butch" than a Dawn Marie, and bore a strong resemblance to her owner. Both Mr. Birdsong and Dawn Marie were built like fireplugs. Neither had been provided with necks.

"They were in the same grooming class and both did well in the relay races. . . ."

Dolores had been in a *relay* race at *dog* camp? thought Lindsey. My *gosh*. It was kind of hilarious, really, but no one was laughing. Of course they wouldn't be laughing. It was a *funeral,* not a party, and you just didn't laugh at a funeral. She still felt very sad and hoped it showed on her face. Then she happened to glance at her brother, who was seated by the stone fireplace across the room. He smiled and flashed her his evil eye.

She quickly shifted her gaze. How unbelievably childish and rude! To try to make her laugh during Dolores's service!

She would not look at him again. She knew that he knew that she had seen his evil eye, and so she appeared as stern and serious as she possibly could. Most importantly, she must not look at him again, not until the service was over.

"... they both loved the food," Mr. Birdsong continued. "It was very nutritious. They ate better than I do at home ... full of vitamins and minerals and all the yummy good things." He patted his ample stomach several times.

Lindsey loved going to camp. She went for two weeks every summer. She especially loved horseback riding. As she imagined Dolores going horseback riding too, the corners of her mouth began twitching.

She lowered her head, focusing on a speck of lint embedded in the snowy white carpet. She must not look at her brother and she must not smile. But even with her eyes closed she could see Eric's eyebrow, floating like a little fish in her mind. She tried to erase the image, to make the screen go blank. Instead she saw Dolores, flying around the corral on the back of a big palomino.

She opened her eyes and lifted her head for just a second—only to catch a glimpse of the evil eye once again. She dropped her head and squeezed her eyes shut. She knew what Eric was thinking—that he had her now. But he did not. She could do it. She could will every cell in her body to stay calm and focused. She must not think about Dawn Marie and Dolores in a relay race. She must not imagine Dolores riding horseback. And she hoped that Mr. Bullfrog would not tell them any more about dog camp. *Birdsong,* she corrected herself. Not Bullfrog. It was Mr. *Bird*song. How ridiculous. She tried to suck in the corners of her mouth to keep them from twitching, and glued her eyes to the speck of lint on her aunt's precious carpet. But darn that Mr. Bullfrog, er, *Birdsong.* . . .

". . . and I think Dawn Marie had a racy summer romance. . . ."

She bit her lip. She needed help and she needed it now.

". . . yes, I do believe Dawn Marie got on well with a good-looking Portuguese water dog but . . ."

It was like a tidal wave and she didn't know how to stop it. Her shoulders began to shake and then her tummy began to quiver. Sandbags to stop the tidal wave, more sandbags!

". . . Dolores, well, poor Dolores . . ."

She thought about Dolores unable to get a date at dog camp and snorted. She dropped her face into her hands but it was too late. Besides, she could still hear Mr. Bullfrog.

". . . she didn't have much luck in the romance department, poor girl . . ."

Lindsey laughed. It was kind of a dry, barky laugh, which she wisely tried converting into a coughing fit. Somebody slapped her on her back, and she laughed again, then sputtered into a few whimpers, more coughing, and one final sob. Her nose was dripping. Her eyes watered. Her shoulders ached. Her head began to pound.

Mr. Birdsong, of course, had stopped speaking. So had everyone else. You could hear the ticking of the old grandfather clock on the mantel and several dogs panting. Aunt Flo crossed the room with a tissue, laying it across Lindsey's lap with a soothing little "There, there, it's all right, sweetheart."

Lindsey grabbed the tissue and blew her nose. Then Tu slid off his mother's lap, bounded across the room, threw his arms around her neck and hung there. She would have run off to the bathroom and remained there until the whole thing was over, but with Tu swinging from her neck like a monkey, it would be very hard to walk.

She had to get rid of him and somehow get to the bathroom. "Don't worry, Tu Tu," she whispered into his ear. "It's okay. I'm not really crying. I just have to go to the bathroom."

"You do?" he whispered back, his face pressed against hers.

"Yeah. I'm okay. Really." She sniffed.

He let go of her neck, jumped to the floor, and clapped his hands. "Hey!" he shouted. "Don't worry, everybody! She says she's not really crying! She just has to go to the bathroom!"

Only now she was crying. She sniffled into the tissue and hung her head.

"C'mere, Tu," beckoned Lindsey's father. "Let's leave your sister alone until she feels a little better, okay?"

It was strange what your mind did in the middle of a

crisis. Hers returned to a seventh grade social studies lesson about the Roman Empire. The Romans had built a huge arena called the Coliseum, in which gladiators fought exotic animals from all around the world. The floor of the Coliseum could be filled with water and turned into a man-made sea. It was amazing. Then the gladiators hopped onto miniature ships and fought sea battles. The arena floor was also equipped with trapdoors, so that gladiators and animals alike could appear and disappear in a flash, to the delight of the crowd. The whole thing was abominably cruel, but Lindsey would have given anything for a trapdoor just then, or the sudden appearance of a horned beast eager to swoop her away.

She sniffled into the tissue as Aunt Flo and Uncle Mo readied the screen and projector for old home movies of Dolores. Then Roger Knipe warmed up his bagpipes. One by one, the dogs began to howl.

Mrs. Green leaned closer and patted Lindsey's hand. "Don't worry. All young girls get the giggles. It happened to me once, at the Miss Lima Bean Contest. . . ."

Lindsey sniffled again. She supposed Mrs. Green was only trying to help, but it wasn't working.

Uncle Mo drew the shades. What a relief. Now nobody could see her and she couldn't see them, and she couldn't see Eric and his evil eye.

There, on the screen, were her uncle and aunt, many years younger, out in the yard with a teeny, weeny Dolores.

There was Dolores romping in the grass. There were her aunt and uncle holding hands. There was Dolores, chasing her tail. There was her uncle, chasing her auntie.

There was her aunt across the room, dabbing at tears with the corner of a little white hanky. There was her uncle across the room, about as moved to tears as a tree.

There was Uncle Mo kissing Dolores; there was Uncle Mo kissing Dolores and Flo; there was Dolores in a yellow beanie; and Uncle Mo and Aunt Flo waving at the camera from a big rock in the woods.

"Oh, how I loved that old dog," sniffed Flo.

"She means me," said Mo, removing the cigar from his mouth for two seconds. A few people chuckled, but Aunt Flo was not one of them. Then the movie was over and Mo got up to turn off the old projector.

"I was on stage in front of hundreds of people," whispered Mrs. Green. "As soon as I said, 'I want to be Miss Lima Bean with all my heart,' I started shrieking. . . ."

"Mm," replied Lindsey, squirming.

"I tried to start over. 'I want to be Miss Lima Bean with all my heart. . . .' "

Aunt Flo made an announcement about the food being ready, and the room was suddenly emptied.

"Please, everyone, watch your crumbs on the carpet!" said Flo, as she circled the buffet table in the adjoining dining room, popping spoons into serving bowls.

"Why?" asked Mo. "What are they going to do? A little jig?" He'd pulled a lighter from his pocket and was standing beside a window in the dining room.

Again, everyone laughed but Flo, who spotted a crumb on the carpet and stooped to snare it like a mad little bird.

Now Lindsey's uncle was *opening* the window. He wasn't going to smoke in the *house,* was he?

Lindsey was still sitting on the sofa in the living room. She'd made a big fool of herself and wasn't hungry at all. She also didn't want to face all those people. She liked sitting there alone, surrounded by the snowy white carpet. It was quiet. But now her mother was heading her way. She couldn't face her mother, either. Her mother would be kind and ask if she was all right, and she wasn't. She'd embarrassed them all and, no, she obviously wasn't normal.

"Honey, are you all right?" Her mom sat down beside her, patting her arm.

Lindsey scrunched up her face and coughed. "I'm not feeling well, Mom. . . ." She coughed again, harder.

"Let me get you something, honey . . . some water, something to eat . . . ?"

"No thanks, Mom." Soon the others would drift back into the living room. She might as well get something herself or they'd all ask why she wasn't eating and pat her on the head like a little Chihuahua. She slowly got up off the sofa. "I'll get something myself." She tried to smile but gave it up and skulked across the room with her head down.

Uncle Mo was smoking all right. She could smell it even though he was standing off by the windows. The end of his cigar was lit like a giant firefly.

Oh, good. Her brother had led the stampede for food and was nearly finished filling his plate. He'd be off to find a seat and she wouldn't have to face him.

She got in line behind Roger Knipe and grabbed a plate from the stack on the table. She would have a little bread or rice to settle her stomach. That was all. She still wasn't hungry. She reached for a piece of turkey, might as well, and one of these rolls to go with it. Skip the potato salad with too much mustard but grab a few of the meatballs. A small helping of fruit salad, a gob of pasta salad, why not, and also the salmon salad, which happened to be a specialty of Aunt Flo's, and one of her favorites. Crackers, cheese, green beans, and almonds. She studied the lasagna. It looked delicious but she wasn't hungry. Oh, well. Just a small wedge and a roll to go with it.

She took a step toward the living room and stopped. She didn't want to return to her seat beside Miss Lima Bean, and forget about Mrs. Philpott and poor Jupey. Forget about Mr. Bullsong, er, Birdsong, too—she didn't want to hear more about dog camp ever again. Roger Knipe was swallowing his food whole—ick—and probably would play those bagpipes. Now she could hear her mother: "Lindsey! Over here!" But she pretended not to hear her. Where was her uncle?

Mo was still smoking by the window. He looked lonely. She felt like going over to him, but she didn't know what to say to him either.

"Mo," rasped her aunt, "that smoke is drifting back into the house. If you're going to smoke, could you please take that cigar outside?"

That's when Lindsey saw the big red ash dangling from the tip of his cigar. She stopped dead in her tracks en route to the living room and just stood there with her plate in her hand. What should she do? She'd better say something to her uncle even though it was really none of her business.

Suddenly Tuesday began to yelp wildly in the living room. "Oh, Tuesday!" sighed Mrs. Green. "Let me at least have a few bites before you tend to your business."

"I'll take her out," offered Mo, easing himself away from the window and making a move toward the living room. "Along with my cigar. We'll all three go for a walk."

"Uncle . . ." Lindsey began in a whisper.

He was lumbering across the room and didn't hear her. That was partly because Roger was playing another dirge on his bagpipes, and the dogs were howling again.

"Uncle . . ." she said a little louder, trailing him in a wake of cigar fumes.

"Uncle Mo!"

Sensing she was about to be liberated, Tuesday had begun to yelp in earnest, drowning out Lindsey's last attempt to avert disaster.

The big ash slipped from the end of Mo's cigar just as he was about halfway across the living room. It seemed to hang in midair for about a half second and then made its descent.

Lindsey reached for the ash with her right hand. She also had a plate of food in that hand, but she forgot that. The plate sailed forth like a Frisbee. She was good at Frisbee. It made a neat landing, right-side up, several feet away. But, due to the laws of physics and gravity, and because the meatballs, pasta salad, salmon salad, crackers, cheese, lasagna, and so on were not attached to the plate, they slid forward onto the snowy white carpet.

She keeled forward, landing on her hands and knees. Uncle Mo was down on the carpet beside her, pawing at a smoldering red eye in the middle of the carpet. A thin curl of smoke wafted upward. But Lindsey's eye was on a fat brown meatball, which had just rolled to a stop smack in front of a pair of dressy black pumps. Her gaze drifted upward, from the pumps to the ankles, up the shapely legs to the hem of a powder blue skirt, paisley blouse, string of pearls, and, finally, the familiar face of Auntie Flo, a face now drained of all color.

Her aunt's mouth hung open. She was looking at the carpet. But now she lifted her head and gasped. Tuesday was squatting on the floor beside Lindsey, doing her business right there in the house, on the snowy white carpet worth twenty thousand big buckaroos. Mrs. Green and Auntie Flo shrieked in unison. Lindsey, still down on all fours, heard a sharp bark from across the room. It was Jupiter, eyeing the meatball. He lunged with remarkable fervor, yanking Mrs. Philpott and her plate of lasagna down onto the floor in a heap.

Now it was bedlam, the room a feverish tangle of yapping dogs and frantic people. Lindsey had begun to crawl toward her dinner, there on the floor several feet in front of her. But it was no use. All the dogs had gotten there before her. She sort of felt like one of them, and had a desperate urge to crawl out of the room unnoticed. But now she saw her mom and dad rushing toward her. She sat back on her heels and burst into tears.

She felt a hand on her shoulder—oh, no, it was Eric. She gritted her teeth against a certain onslaught of ridicule but—what was this? Don't worry, he was saying, as he helped her up off the floor. It's all right. Don't worry about anything. She'd been certain it was Eric, but now, as he led her out of the room, she was not.

"Are we still normal?" asked Tu on the ride home.

"Yes," replied Lindsey's mother, with a huffy little laugh. "We're really, really normal."

"Is Eric still normal?"

"Yes," said her father. "Eric's normal, we're all normal. Dog camp," he added. "I had no idea."

Lindsey glanced at Eric beside her in the backseat. She still couldn't believe that he'd been so kind, getting her out of that room. "Things like that happen," he'd said, slinging his arm around her shoulder as they went for a walk in the neighborhood.

"Not to me," she protested. "Nothing like that's ever happened to me before. I think I might die."

"I shouldn't have made you laugh," he admitted.

Who was this guy anyway? An imposter? He was so nice it was nearly affecting her nerves. If people were going to change that much they ought to warn you.

"What am I going to do about the carpet?" she asked now, leaning forward in her seat. "I only have about . . ." She began to sniffle again, and dabbed at her nose with a balled-up tissue.

"Don't you worry." Her mom turned and smiled. "We'll talk to Aunt Flo and Uncle Mo and everything will be fine."

"They're rich," said Eric.

"Eric," said her mom.

"Relay races," mumbled her dad. "I had no idea. . . ."

★   ★   ★

Tap . . . tap . . . tap. Lindsey lobbed the ball toward the basket. It hit the backboard, *klunk,* but still dropped through the hoop, *swish.*

"Good," Eric cheered, going up for the rebound. "That's a difficult shot."

"Is it?" she said. "Thank you."

It was odd, playing basketball out there in the moonlight, ten o'clock on a Sunday night. She could kind of see why he liked it. Each time she sent the ball sailing toward the basket, the ruined carpet seemed to drift further into the background of her mind. No wonder it was a popular game. It was kind of calming her nerves. In fact, it was the calmest she'd felt in several days.

She caught his pass and positioned herself for a shot. *Tap . . . tap . . .* The ball rose in an arc toward the hoop, an orange pumpkin against the moonlit sky. *Swish.*

"Nice shot. Hey, it's my turn."

"I still can't believe you *(tap)* were so nice to me *(tap)* this afternoon," she said, keeping her eye on the hoop. *Klunk.*

"My turn," said Eric. "Why shouldn't I be? You're my sister." He grabbed the ball and went up for a layup. *Swish.*

He was a good ballplayer, and if she pretended she was seeing him for the first time, then, well, he was sort of good-looking. She wondered if she'd underestimated him in other ways too. *Tap tap klunk.* Maybe he did have feelings. Maybe he was somebody she could almost look up to.

"I used to think you were too much of a jerk to get a girlfriend," she suddenly blurted, planting her hands on her hips. "I think I was wrong. You'll get a girlfriend all right. You just wait and see."

"I will?" he said. *Tap tap swish.* "Good-looking or what?"

She wasn't going to press her luck. What she saw here was potential, and that was enough.

It was too late to do anything about her room, which was still a shambles. She pulled the blanket off poor Cousin Dolores and shoved it under her sleeping bag for extra padding. Dolorosaurus Rex, doomed for extinction.

So that was that, she thought as she slipped into her sleeping bag. Her brother was not the unfeeling clump that she thought he was, and she was the slob, not him. But Dolores was still dead. Poor Dolores.

Her brother was still playing ball in the driveway. It didn't bother her this time. It made her feel sort of good, knowing he was around, knowing maybe he was someone she could count on.

She gazed up at her creation in the corner. She hoped it would not frighten her again in the morning. As soon as her head hit the pillow *(klunk)* she was asleep.

THE YEAR OF THE PIG

· · · · · · · · · · · · ·

He didn't quite believe what he was seeing, a pig trotting down the middle of the street, as though Broadway Avenue were a field in Kansas. This was not one of those little pot-bellied pets on a leash either. This was a big pig, a porker.

"Look at the way it's zigzagging through traffic," said Sam. "I think our quarterback could use a few pointers from this guy." Sam was Eric's best friend and his fishing buddy. In fact, they were on their way to Lake Chabot up in the hills. It was only a half hour away, about as far as Eric's parents would let him take the car. He was sixteen and a new driver. It was a warm, sunny Saturday in late February, and Eric could hardly wait. He eased his mother's Sentra to a stop and shifted to neutral.

"Ever see anything like it?" asked Sam.

"No, I haven't," said Eric. "I just hope it doesn't get hit."

"You know, it kinda fits." Sam yawned and rubbed his eyes. It was only about eight in the morning.

"What fits?" asked Eric.

"That pig running down the middle of the street. According to the Chinese calendar, this is the beginning of the Year of the Pig. Actually, it began last week."

"Is that so?" said Eric absentmindedly. "The Year of the Pig . . ." He hit the brake, as traffic on Forty-first Avenue suddenly came to a halt.

"Well, every year is represented by a different animal. You know, last year was the Year of the Dog."

"Actually, I don't know."

"Well, there's the Year of the Horse, the Year of the Rabbit, the Year of the Snake—"

"That sounds like a good one."

"—the Year of the Rat and so on. It's a twelve-year cycle."

Sam's mother was Chinese, so it fit that he knew this.

"So, like, if you were born during the Year of the Pig," said Sam, "you're supposed to have a lot of characteristics of that animal." Rolling down his window, Sam leaned his head out to get a better look at the situation up ahead.

"So all the babies born this year will turn out to be a bunch of slobs? Is that it?" Eric asked, sighing. He was in a hurry to get going and didn't appreciate the delay.

"Not exactly. Pigs are actually intelligent and generous. You're probably not one of them."

"Thanks a lot."

"What direction does your house face?"

"I don't know," said Eric. "Who cares?"

"I think it faces east, and that could be trouble in the Year of the Pig. A bad omen, according to Chinese tradition."

"So far I can't complain," replied Eric. "I don't believe in that stuff anyway."

"It's only February. A lot of things could happen."

There was a loud screeching of brakes, signaling a possible change in Eric's fortune, and then . . . *bam*. Smacked from behind, the Sentra lurched forward, plowing into the bumper of the car just ahead.

"Aaaaaaahhhhh." Eric dropped his head into his hands and groaned. "I can't believe this. I really can't." Then he turned to glare at Sam, not subtly suggesting it was somehow his responsibility.

Sam shrugged. "Sorry."

"My parents are going to kill me. You know that, don't you? And forget about getting the car again. Ever. That's out." He shifted into park, turned off the engine, pulled up the parking brake, and heaved his shoulder against the car door. As he slid out of the front seat and slouched toward the back bumper he got his first glimpse of the girl running up the sidewalk just behind them.

She slowed her pace as she passed by their car, turned her head, looked right at Eric, and smiled. Then she did this cute little thing. She turned down the corners of her mouth as though to say she was sorry about his car—and she didn't even know him!

He smiled in spite of his predicament, shrugged his shoulders, and watched as she came to the corner and stopped. As he crouched to examine the dent in the bumper, he was joined by Sam and a grumpy-looking guy in a dark blue business suit, who mumbled some sort of an apology.

It was a small dent—and small consolation. Eric slipped the guy's business card into his back pocket and went around to the front of the Sentra to check the front bumper.

"My parents are gonna kill me," he moaned again, sliding back into the front seat with a sick feeling in his stomach. "And I'll have to pay the deductible. It'll probably be hundreds of dollars. What'll I do?"

"They'll make you pay the deductible first," said Sam, pulling the passenger door shut. "Then they'll kill you. And then they'll call the guy who hit you. He looks like an undertaker, maybe trying to drum up some business."

"Thanks." Eric turned the key in the ignition and revved the engine. "That girl running in place on the corner. You know her?"

"No. Like to, though." He stuck his head out his window.

"Sam, please don't act like a jerk."

"I'm not. I'm just going to . . ."

"You're just going to say something stupid and rude, like 'Hey, there, baby!' Get your head back inside."

"I was not!"

"Say a word and I'll dump you off and go fishing alone."

"Okay, okay, take it easy. You don't even know her."

At that moment an Animal Control van pulled into the intersection, followed quickly by an Oakland Police Department patrol car with its lights flashing.

"Ooooh, they mean business," snorted Sam. "That'll stop the poor pig for sure."

The pig scooted in and out of traffic, trotted for a while alongside the road, then turned and headed back in the same direction. It seemed tired and confused. The girl was still standing on the corner, hands on her hips and shoulders heaving. Long brown legs, yellow running shorts, hair pulled back in a sort of ponytail. Hair the color of . . . potato chips . . . no, darker, thought Eric, like peanut brittle.

"I hope it doesn't belong to somebody," he mumbled.

"I doubt it. She has that wild and free look, if you want my opinion."

"The pig, Sam. I'm talking about the poor pig." He shook his head, half wishing he'd invited his grandfather to go fishing instead.

"Ohhh, I thought . . . Well, I doubt it. The pig's probably on its last romp before it goes to market."

"Ugh. Poor pig. Almost enough to make you a vegetarian, isn't it?"

"Not me. I'm looking forward to a couple of Polish dogs later on. So cut with the 'poor piggy.' It'll ruin my appetite."

At the direction of an Oakland cop now standing in the middle of the intersection, the traffic was moving. As they were about to cross Broadway, Eric snuck a last side-long glance at the girl. She sprinted through the inter-section without any trouble, whereas the poor pig, confused and exhausted, had gotten itself trapped by two officers from Animal Control and one from the OPD.

The girl he was to see again. The pig he was not.

So began the Year of the Pig.

Eric set his day pack down on the sidewalk and rolled up his sleeves. It was lunchtime and the quad was packed. He glanced around for familiar faces. "Hey, Steve . . . Wiggsy. How's it going?" He nodded and smiled. Then he picked up his pack and ambled across the quad toward a bake sale, jangling the change in his pocket. Change was all he had because he had to pay half the deductible on the car insurance, fifty dollars, even though the accident wasn't his fault. It was part of being a responsible driver, so his parents had informed him. It was going to be hard to come up with fifty dollars. He was always broke as it was.

There were three oblong tables piled high with baked things—cookies and pies and cakes and nut breads. Good, he was still hungry, but he didn't think he could buy much. He envisioned a big piece of choco-late fudge cake as he headed toward a sign that said BAKE SALE—YOUR LUNCH MONEY FEEDS A FAMILY OF FOUR.

The cake was a dollar. He had eighty-five cents in change. He felt a little sorry for himself because the acci-dent wasn't his fault, and now he'd have to settle for two chocolate chip cookies. He had a sweet tooth the size of an elephant tusk. That wasn't his fault either.

He planted himself in front of a table and dug for change.

TWO COOKIES FOR FIFTY CENTS OR FIVE FOR A DOLLAR, said a small handwritten sign. A girl sitting behind the table was reading a book.

"How much for three?" he asked.

She lifted her head. "I don't know. Let's see. Two into fifty is twenty-five. Twenty-five each then, so seventy-five cents for three. Nobody's asked that."

It was *her*. The girl he'd seen running on Saturday!

He dropped his head and squinted at the change in his hand. His mind went blank. His face got hot and red.

"You want three then?" She was looking right at him—he could feel it. Did she recognize him? No, of course not. He licked his lips and shuffled his feet in the stubby sunburned grass.

"Yoo hoo," she said. "Big decision, or were you just wondering?"

"No, no, I was just . . . I'll take three of 'em." He handed her seventy-five cents, wishing he could explain why his contribution to a good cause wasn't bigger. It would sound dumb, though, unless she remembered him, and he was sure that she didn't.

"That'll take care of the dog," she said, dropping his three cookies into a bag.

"What?"

"The family of four. The dog has to eat too."

"Oh, oh, yeah." He looked at her deadpan expression and wondered. Was it a joke? Was he supposed to be laughing? "The dog," he said finally. "Ha ha."

She lifted her eyebrows. He shrugged his shoulders. It was sad, because he was usually so funny. But not now. He couldn't think of another thing to say about the dog.

"Well, great," she said, smiling. "Thanks a bunch."

He felt dismissed, and knew a quick exit might have been in his best interest, but he remained standing in front of the table for several seconds, trying to think of something to say. Something that would catch her attention, make her laugh, make her remember him. But his pistons weren't firing. He shrugged again and sort of grunted. *Grmph.* Like a pig. It was all he could manage.

He thought about the dog all the way to Mr. Tree's physics class in Building C. Mr. Tree said that timing was everything, one of the most important principles of the universe. So Eric was careful not to step in a pothole, not to trip over somebody's foot and further embarrass himself, in case she was watching. He wouldn't want her to think him both dull *and* clumsy. By the time class had ended, he still hadn't thought of one single funny thing to say about the dog. He was in shock. He'd blown his big chance.

Eric felt a thump under his seat and turned. It was Molly Burton, convulsing in silent laughter in the row behind him. She'd made a little paper hat and stuck it on the head of the guy sitting next to him, snoring in his sleep. Eric smiled and turned toward the front of the study hall, then pulled a copy of the *Banner*, the school newspaper, from his backpack.

Right away he felt a lurching sensation inside his chest. Wow! It was a picture of that girl, the week's subject of SPOTLIGHT ON . . . He read the first sentence: *Shellee Somerville has an obsession,* and lifted his head. He felt funny, guilty, like he was spying on her or something. After all, she didn't know a thing about him.

Mitch was still snoring. The girl on his other side was reading. Nobody was paying attention. He lowered his head and read on.

> Shellee Somerville has an obsession. Correct that. She has two. Long-distance running and feeding the hungry. At first glance you might not see a connection. There is according to Shellee, a senior and a recent transplant to the Bay Area from Calais, Vermont. "They both require you go the whole distance," says Shellee. "It's easy to see how that applies to long-distance running, but it also applies to feeding people who are hungry. You can't do it some of the time. You can't say I'll collect canned goods for a shelter and forget to show up. You have to follow through. You have to dedicate yourself if you're going to make a difference."

A senior, he mumbled to himself, lowering the paper. Too bad. He also learned, in the succeeding paragraphs, that Shellee Somerville was a vegetarian, a member of the cross-country team, that her favorite color was yellow (he remembered her running shorts), the person she most admired was Jimmy Carter, her favorite food was chocolate, favorite group was the Ample Pimple (Ugh! He hated them!), and she hoped to get into Stanford University in the fall.

Wow, he mumbled under his breath. She was not only good-looking but intelligent and dedicated. He felt suddenly in awe of her and strangely elated. But would he ever see her again?

Brrrrnnnnngggg. The bell interrupted both his thoughts and Mitch's nap, as Mitch's head jerked forward, and the paper hat tumbled from his head onto his lap. He opened his eyes. "Wow," Mitch said dreamily. "Who's *that?*"

Eric glanced at the hat in Mitch's lap, fashioned from a page of the weekly *Banner.* "It's Shellee Somerville," he announced with great pleasure. "I know her." Then, stuffing his own copy of the *Banner* into his backpack, he squeezed out of the narrow row of seats into the aisle.

He reread the article later that afternoon, sprawled across his squeaky twin bed, tossing a series of chocolate-covered raisins into his mouth at regular intervals. When he was done he placed the *Banner* on the second shelf of his bedside table, on top of his tattered copy of *Best Places to Fish in Northern California.* He slipped out of his school clothes and into his gray sweats, and stopped in the bathroom on his way out to shoot a few baskets.

He faced himself in the mirror, turning his head first to the left, then to the right. He wanted to see what he looked like to somebody else. It was hard. Hard to be objective. He knew it wasn't a phenomenal face. Not drop-dead good-looking, but not bad either. He closed his eyes, waited a few seconds, and opened them again. He had good skin, no pimples. That he attributed to the switch from Junior Mints to chocolate-covered raisins. Less sugar. He tossed one up into the air, positioned his mouth underneath it, and—bingo.

He watched himself chew. His ears moved when he chewed. Mr. Tree claimed that the ears were merely extensions of the brain, stuck out there in the world. Psychoacoustics, he called it. "So those of you worried about the prominence of those particular appendages can feel absolute pride. You've got ample material to work with." When he said that, he was looking, Eric was sure, right at him. Well, his ears *were* big.

He tugged at his right earlobe—part of his brain. It gave him the creepies.

Anyway, it was his face for life, and he couldn't do much to change it. This made him feel sort of comfortable inside, and also a little depressed. He'd go all through high school with this face. Any girl who might want to go out with him would see this face if and when they kissed good night. He'd dated a girl for two months last year, until she'd moved to Texas. Bad timing.

Cocking his head to one side, he winked at himself in the mirror. "Great cookies. You make 'em?" Well, he'd better work on his personality, too. And finish his homework.

A number of good things happened in the following weeks. First, Eric discovered that Shellee Somerville had fifth-period lunch, same as his. This meant he got to see her nearly every day. It gave him a good feeling just being in the same room with her, knowing he could lift his head and look right at her. He got to see how she looked and what she wore, and, if he passed by her table on his way to pick up a packet of ketchup for his sandwich from home, he got to see what she had for lunch. (She always had egg salad on Friday.)

He hated ketchup, but it didn't matter. He'd squirt a drop onto a corner of his sandwich, just in case anybody at his table was paying attention, or stuck the packet into his backpack. Sometimes he also went back for a napkin, a fork, or another soda. She never seemed to notice him and that was okay—for now.

He had a feeling about this girl. Something big was going to happen. The signs were all there.

Once he found a crumpled piece of paper on her table at the end of the period. With as much nonchalance as he could muster, he grabbed the wad of paper and strode toward the exit. Back at his locker, sporting a growing mound of little packets of ketchup, he pulled it from his pocket to examine. It belonged to Shellee Somerville, a graded chemistry quiz in her handwriting.

Maybe he should've returned it. It wasn't his after all. But he didn't. Her quiz ended up on the second shelf of his nightstand, along with a new tape by Ample Pimple. He'd always hated Ample Pimple, especially the whiny lead singer, Drew Didn't. But he'd bought a tape out of curiosity and now they'd begun to grow on him. You could say Shellee'd begun to grow on him too, but that would be wrong. He was hooked from the first moment. Now he thought about her all the time, floating in a big bubble of good feelings.

He was in the big bubble when he ran over his mother's computer. He was supposed to take it to a repair shop on Broadway and pick up ground beef at the Stop 'n' Shop supermarket. He'd set the computer down on the driveway behind the car, returned to the house for his wallet, got back into the car, and then began to back out of the driveway.

There is a particular sound a computer makes as it is being crushed by a large radial tire. It's like the sound of a very large beetle being caught underfoot.

"I said *run it over* to the repair shop," his mom said later. "Not *run over it*."

Running over the computer was a serious matter, even more serious than the car accident. He took the mangled thing to Bill's Computers, where he was informed by the technician that tire tread on the keyboard was a very bad sign. As if he didn't know.

A half hour later, he was standing in the checkout line at the Stop 'n' Shop, nervously chewing a fingernail, when he saw Shellee Somerville in the line right next to him. His heart began a wild drumbeat inside his chest. Would she remember him this time? He looked down at the package of bloody red meat in his hand and recalled that she was a vegetarian. Tucking the package under his arm, he scooted back to the meat counter, tossed the ground beef back, then grabbed a box of fish sticks from the frozen-foods section. He hoped the fish would please both his mother and Shellee.

When he returned to the checkout line, Shellee was on her way out. He resisted the urge to wave the box of fish sticks over his head. "See," he wanted to holler, "I'm nearly a vegetarian myself." But she never turned around, slipping through the big double doors with her bag of groceries.

His mom wasn't at all happy. She refused to make a meat loaf out of fish sticks and sent him back to the store. She did listen to his soliloquy about the benefits of vegetarianism, then she said he could pay for the fish sticks with his own money and eat them every night if he chose to. He thought that he would become a vegetarian very soon but he had three helpings of meat loaf that night, because it was his favorite food.

It was on his return trip to Stop 'n' Shop that he noticed the pair of two-tone chocolate running shoes in the window of Herbert Kessler's Chocolate Shop. They were the cutest things he'd ever seen, and they reminded him of you-know-who. He needed every penny he had to pay for the car, and now the computer, but he couldn't resist. His whole future might rest on those shoes. Besides, they were only $3.50.

He had a plan for the little chocolate running shoes: get to fifth-period lunch early and place the plastic box containing the shoes on Shellee Somerville's table with an anonymous note: *To Shellee, From ?* He enacted the plan on the following day, but lost his nerve at the last second. Before she entered the lunchroom, he grabbed the box from the table and charged through the herd of hungry kids stampeding his way.

"You schmuck," he mumbled to himself. "You turd brain, you . . ." What a stupid idea. What a lame-brain thing to do. If she'd caught him monkeying around at her table, she'd have thought he was a weirdo sophomore. He *was* a weirdo sophomore, a big coward too, the biggest weirdo coward sophomore in the school.

Forget lunch. Forget Shellee Somerville and the little stupid chocolate running shoes. He pushed his way through the crowd with his head down.

Thunk.

"Ouch."

He looked up, into the startled face of Shellee Somerville. "Oh, 'scuse me," she said brightly.

"S-sorry," he mumbled, blushing and stuttering.

"My fault," she said.

"No, m-my fault." He bent to retrieve the box containing the chocolate running shoes, which had slipped from his hand. "I was going th-the wrong way. . . ."

"Oh, God! Are those cute!" she exclaimed. "Those little shoes are so cute! They're not chocolate, are they?"

He nodded, gazing at the box in his hand. "They . . ." He couldn't think of what else to say.

"Cute." She was looking right at him when she said it. Then she said it again. "Really cute." She reached for his arm and squeezed it.

He blushed down to the roots of his hair and tugged at his earlobe (brain matter!). He ought to say something but what?

Then she smiled again and slipped past him into the crowd.

He ate his ham sandwich at the A & W. If he became a vegetarian it might be the last ham sandwich he ever ate, so he savored every bite. He was glad to be alone, to go over what happened. He still felt the heat of her hand on his arm. "Cute," he heard her say. *Cute.* He could talk to her. You bet he could. Now he was close to getting to know her. You bet he was. Someday he would tell her how the chocolate running shoes were intended for her all along. She would grab his arm and squeeze it like she'd done today, and then she would . . . He looked down at his watch. He was late for his class!

After school that day he set the box of chocolate running shoes on his nightstand, right alongside a tape by Ample Pimple, her chemistry quiz, and the article from the *Banner.* He liked to keep all of her things together. He had to shove his fishing book and a small container of sinkers and bobbers under his bed. He didn't have time to go fishing anyhow. He was running instead. Also too busy thinking, planning, dreaming—and listening to Ample Pimple. They were his favorite group now, and "Burn Your Teeth" his favorite song:

> *Bring me beef, and I'll burn your teeth.*
> *Bring me flowers, and I'll devour.*
> *Bring me a mirror, I'll disappear.*
> *Bring me a pound, I'll pet your hound.*
> *Bring me a dish, I wish, I wish.*
> *Bring me a feather, what feather is leather.*
> *Bring me a fish, your wish, your wish.*
> *Bring me a mink, your house I'll sink.*
> *Bring me cheese, I'll wheeze I'll wheeze. . . .*

A pound of what? he'd wondered, until he realized they were British. Also probably vegetarians and maybe Drew Didn't had asthma. It was nothing like the poetry in Mrs. Fenstemacher's class.

A few weeks later, when the sun slightly shifted its trajectory across the early spring sky, the little chocolate running shoes took a direct hit and melted. Now they were a chocolate running shoe. He was sad, but it wasn't the end of the world.

Sam, meanwhile, was begging him to go fishing. His grandfather was after him too. They didn't seem to realize that he'd changed, that he was no longer interested. Fishing seemed stupid. It seemed like a waste of time, a big zero, a part of his old life, his boyhood or something. He'd rather go running. If he started training hard and went out for track, maybe he could get a scholarship to Stanford.

There were only two Somervilles listed in the Oakland phone directory: an L. Somerville with no address listed, and a Gordon Somerville at 2323 Cheshire Road. That was only about seven blocks away, and he hoped—oh, how he hoped—that that was the one.

One Thursday afternoon in early April, he decided it was time. He picked up the phone and dialed Gordon Somerville's number.

"You have reached the Somerville residence but, alas, no one is home. You can leave a message for Sally, Don, Shellee, Molly, or Paprika at the sound of the beep."

Bingo! He pushed the disconnect button before the beep, afraid the pounding of his heart would somehow be recorded. Then he surged down the hall toward his room, pulled a pair of clean sweats from the bottom drawer of his dresser, and retrieved his running shoes (canvas, not chocolate) from under his bed. He found a pack of Life Savers under there too, pried a red one and a green one free with his thumbnail, and slipped them into his mouth. Then he forced his size eleven feet into his blue-and-white running shoes and took off.

He pounded down the front steps two at a time, and broad jumped onto the wide white sidewalk sparkling in the late afternoon sun. When he was younger, he'd imagined all that shininess came from millions of diamonds embedded in the cement, and it seemed like a magical thing. His life seemed like a magical thing again now.

Man, it felt good to be alive on a day like this. The rush of the sweet spring air in his lungs, the blood pumping through every vein in his body. He was running to Shellee Somerville's house! Then he remembered something Mr. Tree had said in physics—that everything in the universe was either moving toward a particular thing or away from it. It hadn't struck him as anything special when Mr. Tree said it. But now, now he could see it, and it wasn't just because he was running toward her house at exactly that moment. It was as if they were on some sort of a path together, the way he kept seeing her everywhere, and the way they liked the same things: running, Ample Pimple, and now he was almost a vegetarian.

Here it was, Cheshire Road, 2367—2365—2363 . . . He slowed his pace so he wouldn't be out of breath when he got to her house. What if she came through the front door and caught him looking? He'd be a dead dog, a dead weirdo sophomore. . . . 2353—2351—2349 . . . There it was up ahead, a tan stucco house with blue trim and a big front lawn, which someone had been trimming. He sprinted by with his head down, his feet flying over a sidewalk littered with dirt and loose chunks of sod.

He whipped around the corner at the end of her block and dropped to his knees, gulping air. Shellee Somerville's house! He'd seen it! After he'd caught his breath and wiped the sweat from his eyes with the sleeve of his sweatshirt, he got up and started walking. Two right hand turns took him back to her block. He broke into a trot . . . 2327—2325—2323.

The blinds were drawn. No car in the driveway—her driveway, her house, her front yard, her purple tulips . . . He slowed his pace and as he passed he swooped down and scooped a piece of sod from the sidewalk. Then he raced away with the clump of dirt and grass cupped in his hands like a fallen baby bird. Her clump of sod!

When he arrived at home, he took off his shoes before he went inside, smuggling the sod into the house in the toe of one shoe. What was he going to do with it? He didn't know until he remembered the plastic container of flies, weights, and bobbers under his bed. He dumped those things into a paper bag and shoved the bag back under his bed. Then he gently slipped the clump of grass into the Tupperware container and placed it on the nightstand beside his bed. He knew it was an odd thing to do, but he didn't care. He had Shellee's chemistry quiz, the article from the *Banner*, two tapes by Ample Pimple, the melted chocolate running shoes, and now a piece of her front lawn all on the table beside his bed.

He showered, had dinner, studied for a history exam, and fell asleep in the middle of the chapter about President Reagan.

He woke up scratching, itchy all over. Poison ivy again? He tossed and turned, hoping to fall back asleep, but finally flew out of bed lest he get eaten alive. What *was* it? Fleas? Bedbugs?

He pulled back the covers. Ants. Three big black ones scurrying for safety. He scratched his head in wonder. How in the heck did they? . . . Then two more raced across his nightstand. There, the container of sod. The lid was off. He smiled and shook his head. Ants from Shellee's front lawn! He pressed the lid back into place, then went to the window and heaved it open. One by one, he carried the little critters across the room and dropped them out the window.

The moon was a huge silvery disk. It looked like you could reach up and pull it down from the sky, like something he'd seen in the movies. He shoved the window up as far as it would go and swung his legs over the windowsill. It was almost midnight. What if somebody saw him, sitting on the windowsill in his Jockey's? So what! he declared under his breath. So what! He felt reckless, and happy.

The thing was, she could be standing at her window too, at that exact moment, looking up at the very same moon. Why not? Things like that happened. And she could be thinking of him. In fact, anything else seemed impossible.

His heart felt huge in his chest, about the size of a basketball. Well, this thing with Shellee was big, really big. He kept seeing her face, kept hearing her say "Cute!" when she was looking right at him. He wanted her to know he felt the same way, only more so.

Sitting there on the windowsill in his underwear in the middle of the night, he knew he was a goner. In love. What he had felt for his old girlfriend was nothing like this. That was like, like, a warm-up, like, like, a starter kit. . . .

He suddenly knew he was sitting on the edge of his life. He was tired of being a weirdo coward. He was ready for something big. He swung his legs back over the windowsill and set his bare feet down on the hardwood floor. He was ready, finally, to follow the dictates of his heart.

He pulled on a pair of sweatpants, wrote a note on a scrap of paper, and grabbed his Swiss army knife from the top of his bureau. Then he climbed through the window and dropped down into the yard. The cool, damp grass tickled the bottom of his bare feet as he clipped a bunch of creamy yellow flowers clinging to the latticed fence.

He ran down the quiet, empty, moonlit streets of his neighborhood, carrying the bouquet of flowers like an Olympic torch. He didn't wonder if he was doing the right thing. Of course it was the right thing! He imagined her in the morning, stepping onto the front porch and discovering the flowers. She would read the note: *To Shellee, From E.* She would close her eyes, tilt her head back and smile, somehow knowing it was him.

It was cold, but he didn't care. Four blocks to go.

Now and then the beam from a car's headlights swept across the street in front of him. Otherwise it was quiet enough to hear the air rushing in and out of his lungs. It was a good sound, that, and the sound of his feet pounding the pavement. His stride was long and easy. Here was Cheshire Road. He crossed the intersection a block from her house. The wind picked up suddenly, and he drew the bouquet close to his chest.

Now he could see her house, dark except for the porch light glowing like a beacon. He slowed his pace, gulped some air. His heart was going bonkers—steady! Steady! He was right in front of her house now, tiptoeing up the front walk.

His hands shook as he tried to prop the bouquet up against the front door. Steady! Steady! She was in there somewhere sleeping. . . . Then there was this sound— what was it? A car door squealing open? The muscles in his jaw tensed as he turned on his heels.

"Hey," somebody called out. "Hey, you!"

It was a girl's voice. The hair on the back of his neck stood on end as he rose to his feet. He could see somebody getting out of a car. The car was parked right in front of the house. He slowly made his way down the front steps—he tried not to run. But this person was coming right toward him.

"Hey! Hey, what do you think you're doing?"

He cut across the front lawn in a slow trot, his heart racing ahead of him. Then when he hit the sidewalk, he broke into a run. *Bam!* Another car door banged shut, and now he heard the slap of heels on the pavement behind him. He dropped his head and ran for all he was worth. When he hit the intersection a few seconds later, he turned and glanced quickly over his shoulder. The bottom dropped out of his stomach. It was Shellee Somerville, chasing him down Cheshire Road.

She was right on his tail. He kicked his heels trying to widen his stride and pick up speed. It couldn't be her chasing him, it just *couldn't* be.

Now Eric's lungs were beginning to burn, and he wasn't sure how long he would last. The blood pounding in his ears nearly drowned out all sound but he did hear a guy's voice: "I'll get him—I'll get him and I'll bust his brains."

Wake up! he cried to himself. Wake up! It's only a dream!

But it wasn't. His throat was on fire, and he had a heavy pressure in his chest, like a heart attack maybe, or a lung that had burst. Maybe he was going to die . . . die . . . die. . . . The word ricocheted in his head as the sweat streamed from his forehead into his eyes. She was closing the gap. He could feel it. She was going to catch him.

He made a sudden diagonal cut across a front lawn, burst up a driveway and into an alley, hurled himself over a row of low hedges, tore across a wide yard, leaped another row of hedges, tumbled onto his knees, staggered to his feet, and bolted across another driveway and into an open garage door. He couldn't afford a second's indecision and he knew it. Dropping to his belly, he scooted sideways underneath an old junker parked in the middle of the garage, just as they came hurtling over the hedge.

He was cornered, cornered like that poor pig on Broadway.

"We lost him. . . ."

He tried to keep himself from panting, to muffle his gasps for air. They were standing right in front of the garage.

"How'd we lose him? We had 'im didn't we?"

"Don't know . . . thought we had him too . . . you get a good look?"

It stunk down under the car. He was facedown in greasy slime, trying not to inhale it, not to breathe at all if he could help it.

". . . a pretty good look, yeah . . . I think so. . . ."

"Some punk breakin' into your house. Can you believe it? I woulda kicked his teeth in. . . . Wait'll we tell your folks. . . ."

"Oh, Jackson," she cried, "you would *not*. . . ."

Their voices began to drift slowly away, but Eric didn't move for a long time. He wanted to make sure they were really gone. He didn't move a muscle for fifteen minutes, until he got a picture of his bouquet of flowers resting against her front door. Then he cradled his head in the crook of his arm and wept. When he was done crying, he slithered out from under the car, then slunk his way home through alleys and shadows.

Disappointment was a heavy thing. It weighed on his arms and legs and head, making it hard to get up out of bed. He told his parents he was sick, and stayed in bed for two days. It wasn't a lie. He didn't look good and he didn't feel good. He was sick at heart.

"Oh, Jackson," he heard her say, over and over and over. He was a big fool for wanting, and a bigger fool for hoping. "Oh, Jackson, oh, Jackson, oh, Jackson . . ." His poor flowers on the porch. *To Shellee, From E. E* for exit, *E* for eject, *E* for the end.

He played each tape a dozen times. He studied her picture in the *Banner,* remembering the first time he'd seen her and every time after, and the time she'd touched him on the arm and every happy moment. He thought about what could've been and how the future was instead a blank screen. *E* for empty. As Mr. Tree said, everything in the universe was either moving away from something or toward it, and now it broke his heart to think that that was true.

It had rained all day Friday and Saturday, but he awoke Sunday morning with the sun streaming through his bedroom window. For a while he just lay there, letting his face bake in the sun. He knew he couldn't lie there forever, but he couldn't think of anything he wanted to do. When he finally rolled over and checked the time, it was nine forty. Next to his clock sat the small Tupperware container with a piece of Shellee

Somerville's front yard in it. He opened it. The grass had turned brown.

He ate a bowl of Raisin Bran. When he was done, he put all of Shellee Somerville's things in an empty shoe box and took it out to the backyard, along with the container of sod. He dug a one-foot hole along the back fence, then placed the shoe box inside the hole and covered it with soil. When that was done, he took the sod from the plastic container and planted it right over the shoe box. Maybe it was too brown, too dead to grow, but what the heck. It was a good idea.

He dropped to his knees, smoothing the ground around the grass, pulverizing the hard clumps of soil between his fingers. There were some things he didn't understand, like how you could like somebody so much and they didn't like you back. How you could like someone so much and yet lose her.

He saw something moving in the ground and leaned closer. Oozing out of the clump of grass from Shellee's front lawn was a big fat red earthworm. He watched the poor thing try to make a break for it, then dug a space around it with his index finger and carefully pulled it free.

Shellee Somerville's worm. If he was superstitious he might think that finding the worm meant something. But it didn't. If he was superstitious he might hope for better luck with girls in the Year of the Rabbit. No, he wasn't superstitious, and he didn't believe much in luck. But if he had a crystal ball in his hand right now, he'd want to know if someday there'd be a girl who would love him back, love him as much as he'd loved Shellee Somerville.

Thanks to the rain there were earthworms every-where, and he began to collect them, dropping them into the plastic container, one by one. Then he went back inside the house to call Sam.

Teacher of
the Year

· · · · · · · · · ·

It was Eric's first real job. He'd helped out in his
Uncle Mo's Pizza Palace when the busboy called in sick,
and he'd spent a few months hauling peat moss and
chicken manure around Sam's father's nursery in
Alameda. But this was different. This was real money,
meaning it came from nobody he knew; and nobody he
knew could say, "Hey, Eric, what happened to that ten
bucks you got from Uncle Mo last weekend? You got a
hole in your pocket or what?"

He'd had it in his mind for a while, to go out and
look for a job. Then he'd had that little accident in his
mother's car. It wasn't his fault but he still had to pay the
deductible. Plus, he was sixteen and itchy for money of
his own, a constant stream he could count on. It didn't
have to be much, but it had to be steady. In his mind it
looked like a thin gold vein running through a big black

rock. He was tired of figuring out ways to get it, and too old for an allowance.

He saw the HELP WANTED sign in the Stop 'n' Shop window on his way to pick up ingredients for his father's banana whipped-cream pie. That sign was located next to another sign in the window: SHOPLIFTERS WILL BE PROSECUTED TO THE FULLEST EXTENT OF THE LAW. He thought that was kind of funny. Were they looking for help to catch shoplifters or what?

"Baggers," said the checker on his way through the line. "They need baggers and stock clerks, I think. Why? You interested?" She gave him a quick and obvious once-over.

He smiled. "Maybe." Not bad looking, but not his type. Too much gunk on her face.

"The manager has an office back in the stockroom. Just go on back if you want to and ask him about it."

He thanked her and, much to his own surprise, strode toward the back of the store with his small bag of groceries tucked under his left arm, his heart thumping a little faster because he'd never done anything like that before. When he popped through the big swinging doors about forty-five minutes later, he had a Stop 'n' Shop Employees' Handbook tucked neatly under his right arm, and the job. He felt an immense glowing pleasure inside him, and couldn't wait to tell his mom and his dad. They'd sent him out for bananas and whipping cream, and he was coming home with a job. As his physics teacher, Mr. Tree, often repeated, most things that happen in life are a matter of timing, good or bad, and don't ever underestimate its importance.

He knew it was an important moment in his life, one that would later merit an asterisk, like graduating from high school or getting married.

He tapped the checker on the shoulder on his way out of the store. "Got the job. See you Saturday."

"You're kidding! Hey, that was fast! Nice goin'." She stuck out a soft pink hand, and he shook it.

On Friday, the day before his first day of work, he opened a checking account at the Wells Fargo Bank down on Broadway. He didn't expect to get rich bagging groceries at Stop 'n' Shop. But, like Mr. Tree said, you had to start somewhere. Even the universe had to start somewhere, big bang or whatever.

On Saturday morning he woke about seven, showered, put on the required uniform, a long-sleeved white shirt and a dark blue tie, along with khaki pants and his sneakers. He devoured the last piece of banana cream pie, washed it down with a tall glass of milk, and threw his day pack over his shoulder. It contained his lunch, kindly made by his mother, who jokingly reminded him not to help himself to Ben & Jerry's Chunky Monkey ice cream, or anything else, from the freezer at Stop 'n' Shop.

As he swept down the front stairs, he turned and waved a quick so-long to his family—his mother and father, his younger sister, Lindsey, and Tu, his adopted little brother—who were clustered together in the front doorway, waving and singing out their good-byes. He swore when he turned away his mom had a tear in her eye. It made him feel as though he were going off to boot camp instead of his first job, as a bagger at Stop 'n' Shop.

Springing down the sidewalk on his ropey long legs, he hoped for two things: one, that the neighbors weren't watching, and, two, that he wasn't going to be a big disappointment to his family.

As he weaved his way through a small armada of delivery trucks at the rear of the store, he tried to wish away the nervous feeling in his stomach. Get a grip, he told himself, as he took a deep breath and entered the store through the door marked EMPLOYEES ONLY. Maybe this was a bad idea. What if he did everything wrong? What if he couldn't bag the stuff fast enough, forgot things, dropped things, or ruined things, and they threw him out the door on his hiney? Then the asterisk would say, "Failed at his first job as a bagger at Stop 'n' Shop." But Mr. Tree said you had to take chances. It was the only way you got anywhere. So Eric took a few more deep breaths and headed toward the manager's boxy little office tucked away in a corner of the stockroom.

His immediate supervisor was a young woman named Sharleen Pike. She presented him with a white apron, a name tag, and a big red TRAINEE badge. "Could be worse," she said smiling. "Could say, 'Student Bagger. How's My Bagging?'"

She led him on a tour of the store, then handed him over to a big bald-headed guy named Moose at checkout number six. "One of our best baggers. He'll show you the ropes."

As Moose began to "show him the ropes," Eric felt nearly swept away by a huge wave of loneliness. All these people bustling around and he didn't know a single one of them. He tried hard to pay attention, hoping his lonely, out-of-place feeling wasn't all over his face. Because he was right back in the third grade: new school, no friends, adrift at sea until he was finally rescued by his kind teacher, Mrs. Diaz, whom he'd never forgotten.

He picked up a brown paper bag and snapped it open as Moose instructed him to do. "Plastic or paper?" he politely asked the customer, then began stacking the canned goods on the bottom of the bag. He'd hoped at least to see the girl with too much gunk on her face, but no such luck.

He felt as if he was starting to get the hang of it when a large frosted carrot cake slipped right out of his hand and landed—*thunk*—on his size eleven blue-and-white sneaker. It was an embarrassing moment and he felt like quitting, wishing those size eleven blue-and-white sneakers would carry him right out the door.

"Don't let it bother you," said Moose. "Next time go for a field goal."

"I was just testing the law of gravity," replied Eric. Moose laughed. Eric was pleased with himself for a quick recovery. He could nearly hear Mr. Tree, his physics teacher, laughing over his shoulder. Mr. Tree had a good sense of humor.

Soon the work became automatic. He picked up speed. "Paper or plastic?" Snap the bag open. Canned goods on the bottom. Be friendly, be helpful. Watch out for shoplifters.

What did a shoplifter look like? Maybe like this creepy-looking guy shuffling through with his hands buried deep in his pockets. See those droopy eyelids and that hideous scar over his right eyebrow!

Not like this sweet old lady with powdery blue hair and a long black coat, who always bought baby food. Bad stomach? No teeth? She never opened her mouth so he couldn't tell, but she always slipped him a piece of butterscotch candy with a dry, cold hand.

And not this friendly person smiling and waving from the back of the line. Hey, it was his mother!

"Somebody you know," said his checker.

"Yep," he replied, blushing. He felt like his eight-year-old self, when his mother had come to watch him play in his first Little League game. He'd been proud of himself then, and, he was secretly a little proud of himself now. He blushed again, nodded in his mother's direction, and hoisted three heavy bags of groceries into a customer's cart. Be cool, he silently begged her, and don't further embarrass me. But she did.

"Hi there," she said cheerily to the checker. "How's your new bagger working out? Is he keeping up with you?"

"Oh, he's great!" replied the checker. "He belongs to you, I suppose?"

He kept his head down, as he felt himself turn red for the third time in the space of a few seconds. After all, he was only bagging groceries, not finding a cure for cancer, not discovering ancient ruins in the Holy Land, not locating a new star in the solar system.

Though he often wondered about what he was going to "become." Standing in the same spot in the checkout line, doing the same thing, hour after hour—it was amazing the places his mind would go. He could be saying, "Hi, howya doin'? Paper or plastic?" but his mind was nowhere in sight.

Like when this old guy in a cowboy hat comes up and plunks one big Idaho potato down on the counter. Now, he stood in line twenty minutes for that. Maybe the guy was lonely, nowhere to go. Maybe broke, and if all he could buy was a measly potato then that was a shame. But that got Eric to thinking about potatoes because Mr. Tree had just told them about a new potato developed by scientists. This new "hairy" potato was able to fight off pests by trapping them in this sticky stuff secreted by the little hairs on its stalks, important research because a lot more potatoes would survive the growing process without pesticides, and that would help to end world hunger.

That was just one example of what he might be thinking about when he said, "Hi. Howya doin'? Paper or plastic?"

And that was Mr. Tree for you too. He seemed to know something about everything, not just the subject of physics. That was one of the reasons kids loved his class. That was why, if they did poke fun at the fact that his name suited him just fine—he was six feet three inches tall with long knobby arms and legs and a long spindly neck—if they did tease him, it was with a great deal of affection.

So one guy spends a quarter on a potato and the next customer checks out with six bags worth about $192. Go figure. He felt most sorry for the old people shuffling through with nearly nothing, and he was friendliest to them. If he ever saw some poor-looking old person come through the line with pockets suspiciously bulging, he didn't know *what* he'd do.

Dozen cans of tuna, bottom of the bag, six boxes of egg noodles, two dozen eggs, careful, careful . . .

He had ideas. When he bagged groceries, his mind was like a conveyor belt and the thoughts, the ideas, the words rolled through his mind like so many cans of peas and beans, so fast he could barely catch and hang onto any at all, here was another and another . . . his hangnail was sore . . . he needed new shoes . . . essay due Tuesday . . . brussels sprouts, waste of money . . . thirsty . . . when was his next break . . . He thought about money, he thought about his friends, he thought about shooting baskets, he thought about the ugly shirt on the checker in the next aisle, and what he would do with the rest of his life.

"Hi, howya doin'? Paper or plastic?"

He didn't know what he was going to be, and he didn't know how he was supposed to decide. Was somebody going to grab him by the collar one day and say, "Eric, you are going to become an accountant." He hoped not. Because he wasn't good with numbers. He liked biology but forget medicine—he didn't like the sight of blood. Nothing mechanical. He wasn't good with tools. Not a cop. Not a chef. And not a bagger at Stop 'n' Shop. He liked history and geology and astronomy. He liked baseball, basketball, tennis, golf, running, swimming, soccer, ping pong, and backpacking. He liked science, he liked ideas, and he liked to read. If he became a teacher—yes, he could admit it—he wanted to teach like Mr. Tree, to *be* like Mr. Tree.

He wasn't sure why he admired Mr. Tree so much. For what? For knowing so much? For being voted "Teacher of the Year" for the whole district? Nah, it was other things, the way he was with people, how he didn't yell if you made a mistake, if something didn't work out. He said scientists needed to be able to try out new ideas. He said it was frustrating to be a scientist because most of what any scientist did was absolutely wrong. So you weren't afraid to make mistakes in his class. You weren't afraid to try something wacky or say something stupid. You weren't afraid to wonder aloud about the mystery of black holes and what was inside them.

"Republicans," Rebecca King had shouted one day. They had a good time in Mr. Tree's class.

Who was talking to him now? He lifted his head. It was his little sister, plunking two loaves of whole wheat bread and a quart of chocolate ice cream on the counter. "Hey, Lindsey. What's up?"

"Hi, Eric. Spacing out? This is my brother, Eric," she announced to the friend she'd dragged along with her, tugging at the girlfriend's jacket. "And this is my friend, Sheela."

He could tell she was showing him off, and he didn't mind it. Everybody needed somebody to look up to, and he *was* her older brother. "Mmm. Going to make some ice cream sandwiches?" he teased, placing the two loaves of bread and the ice cream in a plastic bag and handing it over.

"Ick!" cried Lindsey, grabbing the bag from his hand. He watched them dash for the exit, then burst through the automatic door, hysterical with laughter. Over what? He shook his head. She was a good kid. He wouldn't shout it from the rooftops or anything like that, but he cared for his kooky little sister a whole lot.

Spying an armada of bread loaves sliding his way, he sighed and pulled a bunch of bags from the rack. He sometimes wondered how many loaves he bagged in one day. How many cans of soup and how many bags of frozen peas, how many rolls of toilet paper and how many pounds of ground beef? People took this stuff home and ate it (not the toilet paper) and turned it into energy, and the energy went out into the universe and . . . now there were about sixty cans of tuna headed his way, and behind them an onslaught of pork chops and apple sauce, oranges and diet soda, Band-Aids and frozen yogurt and instant potatoes . . . stuff, stuff, stuff, and it all reminded him of the first essay he wrote for Mr. Tree's class.

"Give me five hundred words on the principle of gravity," Mr. Tree had said way back in September. Heck. He had racked his measly little brain pretty hard and still had only come up with thirteen! "Gravity is the glue that keeps things stuck to this poor old planet." He finally deserted the project for an A's game, then forgot about it until McGuire blasted a towering homer over the left-field fence. Eric watched the ball go up and he watched it come down, and then he found himself wondering why the ball didn't keep on going. Sure, it was gravity, but didn't gravity ever make a mistake? Couldn't one ball out of a hundred thousand or ten million just keep on going? One never did. It was amazing, a staggering thought when he really got it.

He had picked up his score sheet and had written the essay on every square inch of white space he could find—right there under the lights in the sixth inning of a great ball game. He wrote about the planet being an amazing ball of mud and rock and earth and water and trees and lizards, bottles and cans, cars, newspapers, computers, tuna sandwiches, pillows, Three Musketeers bars, spaghetti, underwear, dairy cows, empty milk cartons, telephones, woolly underwear, CDs, stoplights and Stonehenge, Timex watches and tortillas, pizzas and squirt guns, bicycles, termites and light bulbs, silos and sunflowers, hospital beds, mailboxes, dead bodies, donkeys, books and shoes, Band-Aids, neckties, bacon, canoes and baseballs all massed together and spinning, spinning, spinning, at a phenomenal rate around this big ball of fire, the sun. *You'd think,* he wrote, *that we'd lose a baseball every fifty years or so, or an aardvark or a laundry basket, but we don't because of this invisible glue called gravity, and the only way we can lose something is by shooting it out of orbit with tremendous power and speed.*

"... Hey, Eric?"

See, right away Mr. Tree had him thinking, wondering about everything he used to take for granted. . . .

"Hey, Eric! You with us?"

It was Sharleen, right here next to him, holding up a box of Fudgsicles.

"Yeah, sorry," he said, smiling sheepishly. "I was thinking."

"Could you check the price on this? It's a six-pack, aisle seven."

"Right." He wiped his hands on his apron, slid out from behind the counter, and headed for aisle seven. Past the big display of chips on sale, now the delicious things in their frozen cages—ice cream in half gallons and quarts and pints and cups, ice cream in bars and sandwiches, ice cream dipped in chocolate and almonds and coconut and caramel and M & M's, ice cream cheap and ice cream expensive, plus sherbet and frozen yogurt and sugar-free ice cream. Here it was, the very end of aisle seven, six-packs of Fudgsicles at $3.89. He opened the freezer door and double-checked—$3.89.

He could see people looking at him, knowing that he worked here, and it made him feel good, important. They would ask him questions, and sometimes he knew the answers and sometimes he had to ask. He liked helping people out and making money to boot.

He swung around the end of aisle seven to aisle six, heading back toward the front of the store. Then stopped. He saw the man's hand and the jar in the man's hand, and the man's hand slip the jar into a Macy's shopping bag.

Out came the hand and then the man extended it up . . . up toward the top shelf. He was tall. His arms were long. He reached for the item and turned. Turned and saw Eric and froze.

It was . . . Mr. Tree.

He ran with no particular destination in mind, first along busy Telegraph Avenue, then down one side street after another. He ran until his lungs burned and his calves ached and the sweat streamed down his forehead and gathered in big patches under his arms and at the small of his back. He didn't know he was heading for home until he turned onto Forty-first Avenue. He slowed to a walk until he came to his own house, then stood there on the sidewalk in front of it, his chest heaving and his head beginning to hurt, a dull ache spreading from his temples to the front and back of his head.

He wanted to go inside, slip down the hall to his room and shut the door behind him. Just kiss the job good-bye and go back to cutting his neighbor's lawn for a few bucks a week. And why the heck not? The world was a stupid and miserable place. He took a step toward the front porch and stopped, still gulping air. What would he tell them, his mother and father? That he was quitting, giving up, a coward? . . . No. He shook his head in silence, then he turned and began a long, slow walk back to the market, where his apron lay in a heap on the stockroom floor. Along the way, he could see Mr. Tree in his mind: standing in the aisle, like a deer caught in headlights. Tears came to his eyes. He felt ashamed and brushed them away.

"Hello, Mr. Washington, howya doin'? Paper or plastic?" Eric smiled, but it was an effort. He was dead tired and wanted to go home.

It had been three weeks since the incident with Mr. Tree, and it still felt as though somebody had taken Eric's universe and scrambled the whole thing up. Dropped the sun and the moon and the planets from a big bowl up there somewhere and let them fall where they may. Who *was* Mr. Tree? What *else* did he do—steal hubcaps?

He hated going to work now. He was afraid that Mr. Tree, like other criminals, would return to the scene of the crime. He was afraid he would turn a corner just like before and there Mr. Tree would be, dumping stuff into a big Macy's shopping bag. Sometimes he was sure he did see him—but so far it was always just another tall guy.

It was tough enough going to Mr. Tree's class. It was like "doin' time," trying to learn about the mysteries of the universe from some two-bit thief. He kept his eyes focused on the blackboard behind Mr. Tree's head, and he was sure Mr. Tree wasn't looking at him either. Hanging on until the end of the semester, wishing for a way out of his black hole of disappointment and confusion.

"See ya, Mr. Washington. Take it easy, all right."

He looked up to see his sister waiting for him by the Coke machine along with her friend Taylor Finch. It was the end of his shift, and he'd promised to give them a lift home. He left his station, dumped his apron in a big bin back in the stockroom, then stopped to pay for the pint of double chocolate-chip ice cream he'd eaten on his afternoon break. (Would Mr. Tree pay for his ice cream? Not a chance in the whole blasted universe.)

He was back at his station, digging a couple of dollar bills from his wallet, when he saw Mr. Tree pushing a grocery cart up aisle number three. Eric froze, his breath catching in his throat and his mouth going dry. He dropped the dollar bills on the counter, mumbled something to the checker, and bolted for the exit.

"Let's go," he rasped, as he passed the Coke machine where his sister and Taylor were standing.

"Hey, what's the big hurry?" asked Lindsey, trailing behind with Taylor as he charged across the parking lot.

"None of your business," he turned to snap, "just get your butt in gear so we can get outa here."

"Okay, okay. You don't have to be so grouchy about it. Geeee . . ."

He threw a quick glance over his shoulder as he slid the key into the lock on his mother's Sentra. No, Mr. Tree wasn't chasing after him so far. Thank God for that.

"I was only asking," said Lindsey, sliding into the front seat beside him. "No need to be rude." Taylor hopped into the backseat quickly.

"Do me a favor and save the commentary." Eric licked his lips and swallowed, checking the rearview mirror for any sign of Mr. Tree. That was a close call. *Way* too close a call. He started the car and turned on the headlights, then quickly shifted into reverse, backed out of his parking space, and pulled forward with a slight peel of rubber.

Bam!

He cringed at the sickening sound of breaking glass and grinding metal, then grabbed Lindsey's shoulder to keep her from lurching forward.

"Oh, God!" cried Lindsey. "You've hit something!"

He groaned, dropping his head into his hands. *No, no,* he cried to himself, this *couldn't* be happening *again.*

"You've hit something!" Lindsey repeated.

"I know I have, Lindsey! You stay right here! Don't either of you move!" He slid out of the car to look things over—small scrape on his own bumper, but he'd crushed the headlight of the other car, a Honda something or other. Rubbing his temples with his fists, he silently cursed, then, crouching on his heels, he did a quick scan of the parking lot. Nobody around. It was dark and, amazingly, there was no one nearby.

"You two okay?" he asked his sister and Taylor, as he got back into the car and slid behind the wheel.

"Yeah, we're okay," said Lindsey. "Is it serious?"

"It's nothin'," he said, as he carefully backed away from the other car, then shifted into first and sped forward.

"Really?" Lindsey whispered hoarsely. "It sounded terrible." She peered out the window as they veered around the other car on the way to the exit. "It looks . . . don't you have to call the police or something?"

"The *police?* Are you kidding? For a scratch like that—they'd laugh at me." He tried to laugh, to show how funny it was, but he sounded like a squawking chicken and gave it up. His hands shook on the steering wheel as he gunned the engine and pulled out of the parking lot into traffic on Broadway. His mind was in a frantic muddle, all mixed up with the sight of Mr. Tree and the crunch of breaking glass. He kept checking the rearview mirror, as though he were speeding away from a crime scene. What had he done, and did he know what he was doing?

"Don't you have to . . . do something?" asked Lindsey.

"Do what? I told you it was just a scratch."

"But I saw it," said Lindsey.

"He's not stopping," said Taylor from the backseat.

With another nervous glance into the rearview mirror, he pulled into the left-hand lane. Who did he think would be following him? Mr. Tree and the Highway Patrol?

"I mean, don't you have to? . . ." tried Lindsey again.

"He's not stopping," said Taylor. "Can't you tell?"

He drove down Broadway toward home in silence, hoping his sister wouldn't ask him again if he wasn't going to do something. After a few minutes had passed, he glanced at her out of the corner of his eye. She had her face turned toward her window, and now he could hear it. Shoot, she was crying. He cleared his throat and scowled in concentration, trying to think of the right thing to say.

"What's wrong, Lindsey? Are you scared?"

"No," she said, wiping her nose with her hand. "I'm not scared."

"It's because you didn't stop," said Taylor.

"Of course I did," said Eric, still scowling. "I stopped and I checked it out and it wasn't that bad."

He glanced at Taylor in the rearview mirror, wishing he could think of a nice way to tell her to shut up.

"What's wrong, Lindsey?" he tried again. "You want to tell me? You want me to pull over?"

"She's just disappointed," said Taylor. "That's all."

Eric let out a huge sigh of frustration. He sighed because Miss-Know-It-All in the backseat wouldn't keep quiet, and he sighed because things kept going wrong and his life didn't seem to be working too well. He sighed because maybe she was right about Lindsey and he sighed because he'd been so let down himself.

"Hey." He reached out to touch his sister on the shoulder, but she kept her face turned toward the window. She wiped her nose again and sniffled.

"Look, I know what I'm doing, okay?" he tried. But it was nothing doing. He knew the signs, he knew his little sister pretty well, and he had a feeling that right now she thought he was a big failure.

He slumped in his seat, the weight of her disappointment pressing down on his shoulders. Oh, he knew what being let down felt like all right, and it made him feel sick inside, that it was his fault she was feeling this way.

He kept driving and he kept thinking. What should he do? Drive back to the Stop 'n' Shop and find the car's owner? What if somebody saw him hit the car and he'd be in deep trouble for leaving? He cringed inside, feeling and hearing the crunch of metal again. He didn't want an accident on his record. He wished there was someone to ask, someone to tell him what to do. And, what if he ran into Mr. Tree? He sure wouldn't ask him, now would he? He bit down on his lip, and tightened his grip on the steering wheel.

He was sixteen years old. He had a job and a driver's license and a lot of responsibility and he felt like he was driving away from it all. *Everything in the universe . . . moves away from something or toward it.* In his mind he saw his family gathered in the doorway as he left home for his first day on the job. He remembered how excited he was and how he wanted to make them proud, not be a big disappointment. He hadn't been, had he? He'd done a good job, until now.

He took a long deep breath, slowing the car for a right-hand turn at the next corner. "Hey, I hope you guys don't mind," he said, trying to steady his voice. "I should've stuck a note on the windshield. In case they want to call me or something. I'd better go back and do that." He felt Lindsey stir in the seat beside him, then turn to look up at him. That was how he preferred it.

The car Eric hit belonged to Mr. Tree. He found that out when he received a note from Mr. Tree a few days after the accident.

Dear Eric:

I was surprised to return to my car at the Stop 'n' Shop last Saturday to find that it had been hit, and even more surprised to find your name and phone number on a scrap of paper on my windshield. You've always struck me as an honest, responsible young man, and now I have proof. Fortunately, I have a very good auto insurance policy with a small deductible, which I will pay myself. Honesty should not go unrewarded. I'm sure you have other uses for the small salary you receive from your part-time job.

Which brings me to another subject, unfortunately that of my own dishonesty. I should have apologized before now. I always meant to, and to explain things. But now is a good opportunity.

We both know it was not gravity that took me down from the pedestal. Maybe teachers shouldn't be up there in the first place. We're just people, after all. We make mistakes. We do the wrong thing. Some mistakes are bigger than others. Sometimes we make mistakes over and over and suddenly realize we need help in figuring out why.

I am deeply sorry, Eric, for letting you down, for the confusion I must have caused. Of course, I intend to repair all my wrongdoings, take responsibility for my actions, as you have done. I hope you will take my word on this matter and trust me again as your teacher.

Respectfully,
Roger H. Tree

So Mr. Tree wasn't a dud after all, and perhaps Eric hadn't been wrong to admire him. He figured it must've been hard for a teacher like Mr. Tree to admit he'd made a mistake, but, being sort of a scientist, maybe he was used to it.

When he figured out what he wanted to say, Eric

planned to write back. In the meantime, now that things were pretty much cleared up with Mr. Tree, and he was no longer worrying about some sort of weird scene happening if Mr. Tree popped back into the store, his job wasn't so bad after all. He knew he wasn't going to bag groceries for the rest of his life. But for now it gave him time to ponder the mysteries of the universe, of which there seemed to be many.

THE MAGIC BOOTS

But was he still mad at her? That's what Taylor Finch was wondering as her gaze flitted back and forth between her brother's face and the television. She watched a churning river swallow up a big blue raft as though it were nothing but a toy boat, then spit it out a few seconds later.

"Oh my God!" said Taylor. "Those poor people! They're going to drown!" She kept saying things to show she was paying attention to the movie, but her mind wasn't on it.

"Don't go ballistic over nothing," said her brother, Toby. "It's only a movie."

She glanced nervously at his face to see if he was mad about something. He was lying on the sofa and she was sitting on the floor at the end of the sofa, near his feet.

He didn't look mad, didn't look anything in particular. But you never knew with Toby.

"But it could happen. For real," she replied with relief.

"Maybe so, but it's still a movie. Could you yank my boots off? I'm tired." He yawned, tilting his head back and cracking his jaw.

She glanced at his boots, at the thick black tread caked with dried mud, and wondered where he'd been. She didn't ask him though. Toby did not like questions. He wouldn't give her a straight answer anyway, so why bother.

She kept her eyes on the television as she tugged the boots off his feet one at a time, then set them on the pile of newspapers underneath the coffee table.

"Yuck. Could you put your feet subwhere else dow," she said, holding her nose.

"Don't mind if I do," he said, bringing a foot to rest on her shoulder, then wiggling his toes in her face. He laughed as she shrieked and tried to shove his foot off.

"Hey, we're missing the movie," she said. "Look. That poor guy's been thrown from the raft."

"Cool," muttered Toby.

"But he's lost his shoes."

"Mmmm hmmm."

"Look. His shoes are sailing down the river without him."

"Mmmm . . ."

She looked at her brother. His eyes were closed and his mouth was open. "Toby," she said, but he didn't answer. He'd always been like that. Talking to you one second and dead asleep the next. When he was asleep he looked so different; the hardness in his face melted away, and you weren't sure it'd ever really been there. When he was asleep, he looked like somebody who could never ever be mad again, never say another mean word.

She eyed his boots where she'd dropped them under the coffee table. Should she or shouldn't she?

"...Tylenol, the drug hospitals use most..."

She grabbed the remote from the glass coffee table and hit the "mute" button. "Darn those commercials," she hissed to herself. "They're always so loud."

Toby opened one eye and grinned. "I was asleep. Just like that."

"I know. You've always been like that."

He rubbed his eyes and sat up, then dragged himself up off the sofa and across the living room to the stairway that led upstairs.

"Where you going?" asked Taylor. "I was just going to make us some..."

"Where does it look like?"

"...some popcorn." She was talking to herself now. He wasn't listening, was on his way up to his bedroom. She turned back to the TV, wondering what had become of the man who'd been thrown from the raft, but they were still running commercials. She flipped through a bunch of channels, then zapped the "off" button. She listened to her mom talking and laughing on the phone in the other room, then leaned forward to sweep dirt from Toby's boots from the sofa into her hand, dumping it onto the pile of newspapers.

Taylor moved up to the sofa, then carefully and quietly slipped her feet into Toby's black boots, bending to lace them tight. She was wearing her heavy white socks but, of course, her feet still swam in the boots. Yikes, his feet were big!

She stood up. As always, it was like magic. How different she felt when she put on his boots. "Cool," she said, trying to walk like her brother. "Cool . . ." She clumped her way across the living room and back again. The boots were heavy, tough-looking, with an inch of rubber grid on the soles. It was like wearing a pair of Michelin tires. They made her feel big, powerful, older, like she could do anything.

She strode around the living room for a while and then took them off and left them exactly as they had been under the coffee table. You didn't want to get Toby mad about his boots—they were his most prized possession. If he ever found her wearing them, he'd probably blow his top and then what? She didn't like to think about it. Instead, she went to the kitchen to finish the dishes.

She'd just sponged the last dinner plate clean when she heard Toby tramp down the stairs, two at a time.

"I thought you went to bed," said Taylor "Isn't it late? Where're you going now, Toby?"

"Out." The door banged shut like an exclamation point behind him.

She watched as he hopped the back fence and disappeared down the alley, then hung her head over the sink of dirty dishwater. Where was he going so late, not even bothering to go through the gate like somebody normal? She held the plate under a stream of hot water and set it in the dish rack to dry.

Next her mom came into the kitchen asking where Toby had gone off to.

"Out," said Taylor.

"Didn't he say?" prodded her mom.

"He just said, 'Out.'"

"Did he go off with Rudy?"

"I don't know, Mom. He went the back way."

"He's not going anywhere tomorrow night. That much I can promise you. This isn't a hotel. Eats and runs, eats and runs. Comes in and swallows his food whole like a big snake and he's off again."

"We were watching TV and then ..."

"Then he took off. I know the story, and it's going to change."

Taylor shrugged, pulling a handful of forks and spoons from the bottom of the sink. It got confusing. She wanted Toby to stay home more too. She also wanted him to be nicer, the way he was before he ran day and night like a wild gazelle, but she didn't want to say stuff that would get him in trouble, didn't want him here fighting with her mom.

When she was done with the dishes, Taylor carried a small bowl of leftovers out back, setting it down on the ground next to the back step, same place she did every night.

"Here, Feather," she cooed, crouching low. "Here, Feather." She called it that because it was so skinny. She'd first spied the poor thing many weeks ago, hiding under a bush out in the backyard. It looked even worse back then, its bones protruding from its flea-bitten rib cage. Light as a feather, she figured.

"Here, Feather." Soon a mewling gray cat with a chewed-up ear emerged from the bushes alongside the tall wooden fence. It had a thin white stripe spilling down the center of its sweet, heart-shaped face. It was still mangy and dirty, but nothing like it was before Taylor'd begun to fatten it up.

"My poor Feather," she whispered, as the cat crept closer. "What's happened to your ear? I bet you're hungry tonight, aren't you? Here you go, mashed potatoes and meat loaf. How you like that, little Feather?"

She suspected the cat had been mistreated. Even though she'd been feeding it for weeks, it was still timid. She couldn't stand the thought of somebody hurting poor Feather. It made her feel sick inside, and mad. Really mad. She hoped that Feather would come to trust her. The poor thing never rushed up onto her lap or anything like that, not yet, but each time she came a little closer. Taylor secretly hoped her mother would let her adopt it.

"Gobble, gobble, gobble," said Taylor, because that's what Feather was doing, gobbling up the food like there was no tomorrow. Taylor knew not to get too close when the cat was eating. Besides, she could hear its little engine purring from two feet away.

"Someday you might live with us if my mom will let you. Wouldn't you like that?"

Feather lifted her head and blinked twice, right at Taylor.

"I thought so. You're a little lonely, aren't you, kitty? Well, that's okay. Everybody gets a little lonely," she explained, drawing her knees close in to her chest. "You can't help it. It's just what happens sometimes. It happens to everybody, even me sometimes. And besides, I'm always here. You can see me whenever you want, unless I'm in school or something like that."

She waited until the cat was done with its dinner, then went back inside.

One thing Taylor liked about her mother was that she did not allow arguing at the dinner table. Had enough of that with your dad, she said often. Still it could put a strain on conversation when you knew a fight was brewing, just waiting for the last bite to be eaten and the leftovers put away. She could tell it was happening now, by the deep scowl on Toby's face, the veins pulsing on the side of her mother's head.

Oh, it was a long dinner. The silence got louder by the second, until the food stuck in Taylor's throat and she asked to be excused. She brought her plate to the sink and hurried across the kitchen and out the back door.

Once outside she didn't know what to do with herself. Try to hear something or not. She wanted to know what was going on and then again she didn't. She picked up a tennis ball, threw it way up over her head and caught it, then threw it higher and caught it again, until the voices inside the house got louder and louder and she couldn't help hearing them no matter what.

"I'm laying down the law here, Toby. . . ."

"You can't tell me ..."

She began to toss the ball against the side of the garage . . . *bam* . . . *bam* . . . *bam* . . . as the twilight began to deepen.

". . . and you better get used to it . . ."

". . . Dad doesn't care if I . . ."

". . . You're not living with your dad. This is my home and as long as you're in it . . ."

Taylor threw the ball harder, catching it with her bare hands as it rebounded off the side of the garage. *Bam* . . . *bam* . . . *bam* . . . *bam* . . . It took a crazy bounce and squirted away, toward the back of the house. As she went to fetch it, she heard another sound, a sweet mewling sound, and turned to see Feather creeping toward her from the bushes.

"Feather!" she exclaimed in a whisper. "You've come to visit, and it's not even feeding time!" Taylor dropped to her knees and beckoned the cat to come closer. "Here, baby, c'mon, sweet baby, it's me . . ."

She heard a loud thump from inside the house and turned her head.

". . . Yer insane . . . do what I want!" It was Toby, crashing through the back door like a wild man, eyes blazing, mouth moving, face all twisted, and hands clenched at his sides. He stomped down the back steps and along the stone path to the gate.

"Outa my way. Outa my way."

She lifted her head, frozen.

". . . friggin' cat . . ."

He was right here, towering over her now. He swung

his foot back and then . . . She trailed the arc of his foot as it came forward, the big black boot . . . back and then up, until the toe of the boot disappeared. Where was it? It was buried in the belly of the cat.

"Feather . . ." The word froze in her throat. Up went the boot and up went Feather squealing, three feet into the air and back down.

"Hey!" Taylor sprang to her feet, and grabbed her stomach as if she'd been kicked herself. "Feather . . ." she whimpered, her eyes filling with tears. "Feather." But Feather was gone, and so was her brother.

She laced the boots tight, her lips pursed, her face a study in concentration. She tied a bow at the top of each boot, snapping each lace as tight as it would go. *There,* she seemed to be saying. And *there.* On her way out the front door, she remembered her house key, and her day pack, which she slung over her shoulder.

She was doing this because he was mean, because he was not sorry.

Marching down the front steps and sidewalk in her brother's black boots, she looked like a girl who knew where she was going—and she did. She would walk the ten or so blocks to her destination, and when she got there she would carry out the rest of her plan.

The boots still felt good on her feet. She felt strong and powerful wearing them, but it wasn't because of the boots. It was because of her own self and what she was doing.

She was doing what she was doing because it was the

right thing to do. It was because he'd changed and she no longer knew him. He'd changed in so many ways and none of them good. If a person changed in too many ways, they became somebody else. That's what happened to her brother. She didn't know why it happened or how it happened, only that it happened. And the truth was, the new person was a big disappointment.

It was early on a Saturday morning and hardly anyone was out on the street. Both her mother and her brother were still asleep, and nobody knew where she was or where she was going.

It didn't take her long to get down to the creek. The first time she came to the creek it was with her dad. He said he was taking her and Toby fishing, and she was surprised to find that there was a creek so close to their home, right here in the city. But when they got there, it was only a dry creek bed, no water, and they'd gone to a movie instead, and bought fish at Safeway.

Things changed. Now the creek ran high and fast. They were having a wet winter. You could only see the tops of the big gray boulders, and the creek water rushing over and around them.

She followed a woodsy path half overgrown with tall weeds and shrub oak alongside the creek. The air smelled good, fresh and sweet, and the sunlight streamed through the canopy of trees, warming her face. You could feel awfully good on a day like this. Once she was through with her business, maybe she would.

When Taylor came to a place that wasn't too steep, she carefully edged her way down the slippery bank toward the creek itself. She didn't worry much about slipping. Her brother's boots seemed to clamp her feet right to the ground.

She found a flat white rock at the edge of the creek and sat down. She was thinking, but not about anything in particular. The creek rushing by made it hard to hold onto a thought. It sort of swept thoughts away and they didn't seem to matter.

A picture came into her mind. She saw herself and Toby running down the middle of the dry creek bed the day her father had tried to take them fishing. She saw them laughing, collecting stones, examining a marooned turtle. Then the picture was gone, swept downstream in her mind.

She picked up a small blue stone and tossed it into the creek, where it was gradually carried away. Then a different Toby crashed through a door in her mind. He raced toward her in his heavy black boots. She saw a boot fly upward, and heard Feather squeal.

Taylor pulled both her feet up onto the rock and began to undo the laces in the boots. She really had only one rule to live by: Don't pick on anything smaller. She removed the left boot, setting it upright on the rock beside her, and then she removed the other. Wriggling out of her day pack, she set it upon the flat white rock and stood up.

Squinting into the pale February sun, she watched the creek rush by, then reached for one of the boots. She was doing this because he was mean, and if he ever got nice again she would buy him the best boots in the world. She drew her right arm back, then flung the boot out into the middle of the creek. *There,* she said to herself. *That one's for Feather.* She did exactly the same thing with the other boot. "And that one's for *me*," she said as she hurled it into the muddy water.

They looked like two sturdy little ships sailing forth on a journey. She watched them bob along until they disappeared downstream, then, sighing softly, she pulled her red sneakers out of her day pack.

Heading toward home, she felt strong and powerful in her own shoes, like she could do anything. Oh, she knew that she was walking toward trouble. By now Toby would be more than wondering where his boots were. He'd be *mad,* and she'd have to face him. She swallowed hard just thinking about it. Then she let the thought go, and let her sneakers carry her along as the creek carried the boots to a new destination.